best wishes

Mike

March '06

DREAMS IN THE NIGHT

Sixteen Short Stories

Michael Morley

Hideaway Publications Ltd

This book has been printed digitally for
Hideaway Publications Ltd
4 Erroll Road, Hove,
East Sussex, BN3 4QG
United Kingdom

Database right: Lightning Source UK Ltd (maker).

ISBN 0-9525477-4-0

Front Cover: From an Oil Painting by Michael Morley

CONTENTS

Death of a Schizoid

I read the report in the Evening Argus. A 25 year-old man called Paul Ditton had jumped from Beachy Head, after arguing with himself on the edge of the cliff. A passing hiker had seen him point at someone who wasn't there and shout abuse before disappearing. The deceased had left a note and the police were not treating the death as suspicious. It was clearly suicide. I decided to offer evidence at the inquest.

You see, Paul Ditton had once been a patient of mine for eight months. He came to me from his GP who had drugged him up to the eyeballs in an attempt to treat chronic insomnia but had made little progress in discovering what was actually causing Paul's problem. It was clear from my first sight of him that, though he was a psychopath, showing a marked lack of social responsibility and an inability to relate to other people, he was not angry or resentful. He barely glanced at me when we first met, offered a limp handshake and sat with bowed shoulders and a demeanour that suggested both lack of self-esteem and a sense of guilt. Yet he was a good-looking boy and when he stood up straight he touched six feet tall. His brow appeared permanently furrowed but there were times when he was able to laugh away the lines and show an attractive personality. There was an intense yearning in his eyes, as if whatever haunted him might eventually be absolved.

At least as a psychotherapist I was able to unravel some of his problems. I quickly discovered that he was living on his own, subsidised by Social Welfare and working part-time at a Convalescent Home for the Elderly. His apartment was wretchedly furnished and his immediate neighbours were not unlike himself, unhappy and depressed about their poverty of means and ends. The tenants were too quarrelsome to become friends and Paul was known to be violent on occasions, particularly in the middle of the night when he felt the need to wander about. He had been threatened with eviction if he played his kind of music after ten o'clock. He

1

told me all this haltingly, nervously twisting his hands. It was his fault, he said, he knew he shouldn't disturb others but he had to do something to stop his mind thinking and thinking.

Thinking about what? There was a long silence as he struggled to express some kind of answer. 'Do you feel lonely during the night?' I asked.

'No, nothing like that,' he replied, shaking his head emphatically. 'I often have company.'

'Your parents?' I was not certain what he meant by 'company'.

He gave a small grimace. 'She doesn't even know where I live.'

'Your mother?'

He nodded.

'What about your Dad?'

A shrug of the shoulders.

'He left years back.'

'Tell me about your mother,' I said.

I expected a diatribe but he launched into a warm defence of a woman who had endured much hardship and deprivation over the years and who had always tried to be a caring mother. Clearly he loved and admired her, though they had been estranged for some years.

'It wasn't her fault,' he said enigmatically.

'You mean it was your Dad's?'

'Not really,' he replied. 'He left when she was still pregnant.'

'Before you were born?'

'Yes.'

This was puzzling. Who was to blame and for what? He seemed reluctant to continue. It took some time before he disclosed the full situation. There were twins and one of them had died at birth. The grief-stricken mother had been traumatised by the death of her first son who barely took one breath of air in her arms before expiring. The second survived without trouble. Peter died and Paul lived on. Who was to blame? Who had wrapped the umbilical cord round Peter's neck and choked him? Why should one boy be saved and not the other? It was evident that Paul, now in his early twenties, still felt some kind of guilt about events in the womb. He was sobbing in my surgery when he fantasised about what must have happened as the twins kicked and turned; it was accidental but fatal and it was all his fault. He seemed to be pleading with me, as if I had some judgemental connection with the tragic death.

I would say that this transference of guilt is not unusual in such cases but it is certainly abnormal for an adult to be so fixated. Something must have caused an obsessive concern during childhood. This was disclosed at the next session when Paul arrived in an exhausted state and lay on the couch too tired to talk coherently. I had to piece together the extraordinary circumstances that surrounded his upbringing, sometimes after waiting patiently while he drifted in and out of sleep. He seemed to be carrying on a conversation with himself, occasionally stopping to argue about details of home-life and his relationship with his mother. I was appalled by what I heard.

She apparently developed psychic sensitivity as she breast-fed her only child, offering the other breast simultaneously; she moved into trances that enabled her to talk to the missing twin, as if trying to keep the baby alive. As Paul became a little older, he grew accustomed to her disappearance under the stairs, into a kind of cubby-hole used to store household cleaning equipment. Cleared of clobber, fitted with a lockable door and lighting, this was transformed into a kind of shrine and little Paul was eventually taken into this inner sanctuary by his mother. There was a blue light shining constantly and he sat on a stool facing a decorative shelf on which various family relics and photographs of Paul at different ages were kept. There was a soft carpet and drapes all round. It was a silent, claustrophobic cell but awe-inspiring. His mother was convinced she could keep in touch with an absent son who in some mysterious way was growing up through various childhood phases like Paul. After visiting the shrine, she would tell Paul what messages Peter was sending him and this kept her happy, though Paul must have felt bewildered and apprehensive. Paul, as he grew older, was sent here regularly to commune with the lost brother, sometimes because he had done something wrong, sometimes when comforting support was needed. He was expected to stay there for an hour at least, listening for any sounds of a presence and hesitantly whispering words. There was a small mirror on the wall. Paul would look at his own reflection until it began to distort, his features moving out of alignment, his eyes beginning to glare back aggressively. There were times when it was not himself that stared out of the mirror, but some one similar. He would talk to this image, call him Peter and try to tell him about his life. The image could scowl and rage, emitting strange guttural sounds. Paul tried to soothe him until he felt he could emerge from the shrine and continue his solitary childhood, which was so marred by the mother's paranoid grief.

Eventually, his mother became so neurotic she was difficult to deal with. She seemed to value her time with Peter, within the confines of the understairs shrine, more than with Paul. She joined a spiritualist group and spent hours in what she called meditation. Days would go by without words between them and he often had to prepare meals. He sought comfort in books from the library and the daily routine at school where he worked hard at exams. He could have gone on to further education but he dropped out, unable to be free of his mental stresses. He quarrelled with his mother, left home and became a drifter, unable to settle to any kind of steady job.

Thanks to my therapy, Paul made progress in ridding himself of the infantile fixation that he was responsible for his brother's death. It was obvious he was innocent of any intention to harm him and yet Paul kept nagging himself, repeating that he was really to blame even though I had long made him accept his innocence. There was some part of him that just would not allow his guilty conscience to rest. He would leave my office smiling with relief, secure in my assurances that he had nothing to fear, and then, miserable and self-critical, return for the next session, persuaded somehow that he had no right to claim the life he possessed. He would like to give it to his brother.

I stopped treating Paul Ditton after he tried to throttle me. During an emotional session he suddenly changed his personality so completely that he was almost unrecognizable, both facially and vocally. Did I provoke him unreasonably? I was convinced that Paul

4

had to confront the reality of Peter's death so I proposed that he should ask his mother where the baby Peter was buried or cremated, and we would then deliberately visit this site and firmly accept the completion of Peter's brief existence. This suggestion seemed to enrage him. He suddenly lunged forward and attacked, forcing me to the floor and trying to squeeze my windpipe. Fortunately, I was able to strike him with a bronze bust (of Freud, ironically enough) that fell off a shelf as we struggled, and he collapsed into unconsciousness. When he came to, he had no recollection of the assault. This schizoid behaviour alarmed me and I sent him for psychiatric analysis at the hospital.

I told the Coroner that I had taken no further part in treating Paul but actually my recovery from this murderous attack was gradual. My nights were disturbed. I began to suffer symptoms of narcolepsy, unable to distinguish between dreams and waking reality, a condition that most certainly afflicted Paul. I would dream that I was unable to breathe, choking as I struggled against a heavy weight that held my face down on the pillow. I felt there was some presence hovering over me, casting a menacing shadow and though I never saw his features, somehow I knew this incubus was connected with and created by my dealings with Paul Ditton. I was being punished because I wanted Paul to deny his twin brother's existence. Something, or someone, was driving Paul to resist the positive progress we were making with my therapy. Gasping for air, shivering with fright, I was aware that suffocation was also reality.

Did the hospital treatment effect some kind of recovery? I know that my horrible dreams subsided and I was able to immerse myself in other cases. By the time Paul Ditton was killing himself while of unsound mind (as the Coroner's report termed it) I had lost all touch with him. Out of curiosity I decided to attend his funeral; perhaps also I intended to say something comforting to his mother, but the chaplain told me she was too ill to be present. It was a totally uninspiring ceremony attended by few relatives or friends. Afterwards, I walked home from the Woodvale Crematorium. Dusk was falling as I went down the driveway, aware of hundreds of starlings wheeling in great circles overhead. Autumn tints touched nearby trees. There was a man standing by a clump of bushes watching me. He wore a dark hat and his hands were thrust deep into his coat pockets. At first I wondered if he had been at the funeral but there was something about his motionless stance that disturbed me. I stood still to focus my gaze. For a moment we exchanged glances. Then he faded into the bushes but not before raising his arm as if greeting me. Recognition was immediate – I knew it was Paul Ditton.

Or rather his ghost. I could not believe my eyes. I had just seen a coffin enclosing the mortal remains of Paul Ditton sliding behind a curtain, destined for cremation. He was dead and his ashes would soon be interred. And yet here was a manifestation – how could it be? – that was like him, or perhaps not unlike him, accosting me as if intent on some kind of communication. I walked quickly towards the bushes, hoping to find evidence of a real person, a tramp or casual visitor, but there was no one. The starlings still arched like a great wing overhead, twittering.

That night I dreamed I was fighting for dear life against a dark oppressive figure whose hands were round my throat. I thrashed about, moaning and trying to press finger-nails into the eye-sockets of this assailant. He howled in my ears as he choked me; I was suffocating to death. And then the pressure relented, the threshing and churning changed direction and I sensed in a flood of panic that a second fearful presence had entered my dream and was grappling with the other, two powerful incubi wrestling over my weakening body. In my dream, under closed eye-lids, I could see two identical faces glaring at each other, hatred burning in bulging eyes as one strained to overpower the other.

Gradually I regained consciousness, sweating and gasping for breath. I sat up and peered into the darkness of the bedroom. The visitation had ceased. I was alone but now I knew there were two adversaries intent on murdering each other and possibly me too. It was a sad outcome for the abnormal efforts of their mother to keep her family together. Clearly there was no love lost between Paul and Peter; they hated each other. What worried me was their attitude towards me. Was I the battlefield upon which they would fight their terrifying duel? I began to stay awake for fear that I might dream and become enmeshed in a struggle that could fatally injure me.

6

Against my will, I was beginning to believe in the existence of this other brother. When my wife, disturbed by my tossing and turning, my moans and sighs, decided to sleep in the spare room, I confided in her. She allayed my fears, she settled my mind. I was overwrought; I was feeling guilt that I had not persevered with Paul Ditton as a patient; I had been overworking and we needed a holiday. She would book a hotel in the West Country at once and we could get away from it all. Thanks to her, I was able to rationalise the situation. I was aware that everyone has a dark side, a reverse identity that is the opposite and complement to one's normal psyche. I began to think my unconscious was trying to tell me something about myself, though I couldn't understand the message. Such complacency was to receive a severe shock.

We stayed at The Headland, Newquay, for a long weekend, having booked a room that overlooked the superb beach that stretched for miles, with the white-crested Atlantic rollers roaring in towards us. We took walks to Fistral Cove and an excursion to St Agnes Head, absorbing the spectacular scenery and relaxing in the warm, fresh air. We enjoyed afternoon tea in the lounge of this old hotel which, perched on a craggy promontory, gave grandstand views of the antics of surf-riders pitting their physical skills against the relentless treachery of the breaking waves. On the final afternoon we occupied our usual armchairs and settled down to watch the entertainment. There was something hypnotic about the rollers breaking quietly and continually as we watched through the windows, a lazy inevitability about each surge of water that seemed to push at the wave in front, demanding that it should break down into foam and spume. The long white line approached until it died on the sand.

And there were the young surf riders effortlessly gliding over the breaking waves, seeming to walk on water. I could not help thinking they were far removed from the tense urban jungle where Paul had lived out his wretched, guilt-ridden existence. I watched one youth as he stood proudly riding the foam, his slender frame shifting elegantly as he swayed over his board, heading for a rift between two conflicting breakers. He reminded me all the way of Paul as he might have been, liberated from his crippling fears and

7

free to enjoy the sun and the sea. Indeed he seemed to be waving to me happily and I wanted to get up and wave back, just to urge him on. And then I saw another surfer, a dark, crouching figure, travelling at great speed, heading straight for him, cutting through the waves on a collision course. In a flurry of spume and crashing breakers, both fell as they met, lost momentarily in the broken waves.

That night I slept badly. There was something knocking outside our balcony and it kept me awake, until my wife ventured out and fixed the ventilator flap. Once asleep, I dreamed I was floating upright in the sea, bobbing about and trying to avoid the dark fishes that darted all around me. It was enough to sadden me for the rest of our holiday, but I retained happy memories and put aside such imaginings as morbid.

One grey autumn afternoon shortly after our return home, I fell asleep over the television programme I was supposed to be watching. My wife, who had watched over my nervous condition during the happenings with some anxiety, had slipped out to post a letter while I was resting. I was woken from my slumber by a ring of the doorbell. I assumed this was my wife returning and, having forgotten to take her front-door key, she was summoning me to open the door. Upon opening the door, I was shocked to find a man standing in the porch, wearing a dark overcoat and a brimmed hat. He did not move or speak, but instantly I recognized that face from my dreams, the gaunt cheekbones, the glaring eyes, the curled sneer. My scalp prickled as he stared, suddenly scowled and tilted his head as if about to speak. A chill breeze froze my body and momentarily I closed my eyes. When I opened them, he had gone like a ghost in a mirror.

Trembling, I shut the door. Who was this visitor? Why was he calling on me? I knew I could not dare to open the door in case he was still there. Of course I did not immediately identify him as Paul Ditton. I could remember features that related to the younger Paul I had known, but there was too much that was different, a malevolent venom in the burning eyes, thinner lips, a sheer menacing presence that belonged to some other personality. And with horror I realised who this must be, however improbable. It was Paul's twin brother who, though separated from him at birth, still existed in some kind of immaterial form and, having kept pace with Paul as he grew older, now was free to roam and wreak his vengeance on the world! With Paul's leap from Beachy Head, the two brothers had been brought into direct contact with each other, with terrifying consequences for me. My attempt to provide psychological treatment had released forces beyond the control of human understanding. This visitor from the shadow world was intent on tracking me down. What happened next I shall never forget or be able to explain.

There was one short ring of the bell, a scream from the porch and a momentary hammering on the door. I rushed to open the door and found my wife stretched out in the porch, gasping for breath and feebly pushing her arms against invisible powers. She fainted as she saw me, relaxing from her paroxysm as if knowing she was saved, but I could see a misty dark form materialising over her, a figure like my malevolent visitor, and his hands were reaching for her throat. There was a screaming in my ears but I couldn't help, I was paralysed with fear, unable to reach out to help my poor wife. And then, like a scorching blast from a tornado that rocked the walls of the porch, another swirling cloud took on a bodily and visible shape and leapt at the surprised assailant, who was thrown backwards violently. Through a haze of whirling mist that resembled arms and legs of two wrestling bodies I could see my wife lying motionless. Back and forth they grappled, shouting and cursing, until one of them was forced to the ground and I could see fingers gripping a throat and squeezing. I watched the horrible face slowly crumbling and disintegrating. The body evaporated and a strange sighing filled the air. One dark figure remained in the shadowy porch and he turned to me ominously, but I could see he was smiling as he raised his arm as if saluting me. I knew it was Paul at last freed from the haunting of his other self, slowly disintegrating into the shadows and leaving no trace of his presence.

It was the last time I saw him. Gently I carried my wife into the house, phoned for an ambulance and tried to resuscitate her. At the hospital she was diagnosed as suffering a sudden heart attack in the porch. When I protested that she had been attacked by ghostly

9

apparitions, no one at the hospital believed me. Even my wife failed to verify my account of her ordeal; she could remember nothing and chose to believe the medical staff rather than me. She was quite content to accept that she was a victim of cardiac arrest. But I know that she, like me, had been involved in a terrifying collision between two worlds and I had witnessed the titanic struggles between two brothers that ended with the final triumph of Paul. At last I am able to sleep in peace.

A Bracelet of Bright Hair

The bracelet would appeal to a hair fetishist, Liz thought, but I'm not that kinky. She looked up to quiz the sharp-nosed elderly customer. Where could he have unearthed a period piece like a hair bracelet? It wasn't up to much; pale golden hair plaited quite neatly but the metal clip looked like pewter. A home-made job from a Victorian farmhouse? Not the kind of thing an aspiring period jeweller could sell easily.

'There isn't much demand for these,' she said cautiously.

'I know,' he spoke with a slight guttural accent, 'but they are surplus to my collection.'

'Your collection?'

'My memorabilia,' he explained. 'I am Karl Schadel.' And he handed her a dog-eared trade card. His name was in Gothic type, and beside a somewhat sketchy draped pillar on the card, the words 'Antiquarian', 'Sepulchres' and 'Funeral Reliques'. Rimless glasses, an untidy speckled beard that concealed his neck, smiling and nodding his head like an old hen in a barn, had Liz not to be on her guard over a haggle, she would have found him quite an endearing oddity. He didn't belong to the Street, that was obvious.

He patted her hand and held up the bracelet. 'Is it not lovely? Golden hair, so fine, twisted and clipped to fit a lady's delicate wrist - like yours. Allow me!'

Before she realised what was happening, he had slipped the bracelet on her wrist. She stared at it and then pulled at the circlet, panicking, as it seemed to tighten like Chinese handcuffs. It made her feel he was claiming possession of her and she was very frightened.

'Take it off me!'

A look of concern spread across his face. He held her hand and gently slid the bracelet off her wrist. Once freed, she could make

11

light of the assault though the cold touch of his fingers lingered. He was apologising, telling her how much he loved hair adornments. He collected plaited pendants, brooches with hair fanned under crystal, ear-rings and tie-pins with curled locks embalmed in amber, but especially bracelets made by lovers for each other, their hair forever entwined in circles of eternity, sometimes centuries ago.

'Love even unto death!' Karl Schadel sighed. 'When the skeleton is exposed, there round the ulna and the radius the bracelet of bright hair is found. What a beautiful symbol of the power of love!' Liz glanced at him, wondering if he was entirely sane. He leant forward and touched her hair with the bracelet.

'I think this Victorian lady had hair very much like your own, my dear,' he smiled and nodded at her. She felt mesmerised.

It was at this point that Derek opened the shop door with a jangle of the bell. Never had she been so glad to see him and he quickly took charge. Firmly, almost contemptuously, he rejected Schadel's bracelet and stood by the door as the old man, clearly embarrassed, scuttled down the Street without taking it. Liz suddenly felt sorry for him. He hadn't intended to harm her, after all.

'Don't waste your pity on that skunk,' said Derek. According to him, Schadel was a vampire who slept in a sarcophagus, a war refugee who ran a business called 'Memento Mori', specialising in funereal relics and antiquities, on the other side of the river. You took the rowboat ferry and once at his mausoleum wandered between ancient coffins, grave stones, epitaphs, votive urns, skulls and marble angels. Nobody trusted him, he was bad for trade.

Liz decided to say nothing about the bracelet tightening round her wrist. Derek would probably blame her for being too emotional. 'You've got to be like precious stones in this job, Liz,' he argued, 'hard and polished.'

He dropped the hair bracelet into the waste bin. There was an auction of some Castellani jewellery coming up at the Salerooms and he wanted her to check the market prices. At least there was a demand for such period pieces.

'Got something different to show you,' he said. He took a packet from his pocket and opened it. There was a tangle of dull black stones of various shapes and sizes.

'Jet!' he explained. 'Lignite, shale, fossilised wood, very hard, takes a brilliant polish - and the best comes from Whitby up north! I persuaded Mrs. Arkwright to part with them, help pay her gas bills.' He picked up a black brooch and rubbed it on his sleeve, then touched a shred of paper. The paper stuck to the jet.

'The real McCoy, washed up on beaches!'

'I thought that was amber, 'she said.

'Same thing, only different, both worth quite a lot. Jet for mourning, thanks to Queen Victoria and her late deceased Consort.' He picked out an intricate necklace of black faceted lozenges, diamonds and ovals, and draped it from her neckline.

'What d'you think of this, Liz?' The delicate segments glowed on her skin, forming a neat pattern. Suddenly she understood the appeal of jet, so simple, direct and clean. 'It's lovely!' she replied.

'Very pretty! Obviously meant for you. It's yours for ever!' And he fastened the necklace and lightly kissed the nape of her neck.

It seemed to Liz wonderful, a romantic declaration of love following his knightly rescue of a damsel in distress. Perhaps it wasn't unexpected, for he had become very attentive recently, almost harassing her at times, but she could hardly refuse his gift. She didn't know much about love but it was certainly flattering to be courted in this way by a handsome older man.

For Derek, in his early thirties, the age gap was an advantage. He could be the mature partner. He knew the value of this gift - it showed his love for her and he would make a comfortable profit from the rest of Mrs. Arkwright's jet jewellery. The point was that once engaged or living together, he and Liz would have access to more capital from her parents. He didn't want to stay in a lock-up shop in the Street for long.

So they planned to marry in the autumn and meanwhile Derek moved into her flat and they ran the shop together, though sales were not as good as they hoped. Particularly no one seemed interested in the jet jewellery displayed on a tray in the window. It was almost in desperation that Derek asked Liz if she would mind

13

loaning her jet necklace so he could enhance the display. Of course it would not be for sale, he pleaded, but it would focus attention on the other items. And it was true, with the necklace as a centrepiece; it became a very attractive display. Far more passers-by stopped to look at the exhibits.

One afternoon, when Liz was out shopping and Derek was quietly working through the accounts in the back room, the doorbell jangled and Karl Schadel entered, wearing his shabby black coat and a beret like some kind of shady secret agent. He seemed nervous and rather put out to see Derek and not Liz in the shop. 'Excuse me, sir,' he said. 'I can resist no longer. I am in love with your jet jewels, please may I examine them?'

Any customer was welcome to Derek and he slid back the panel and removed the tray from the window. Schadel immediately lost his unease as he bent low to examine each piece in turn.

'Exquisite! The workmanship, the shaping, the polishing - how these black stones glow, like dark flames in the night! Dark, dark, dark, in the blaze of noon eh!' he exclaimed.

Derek waited patiently. The antiquarian was drivelling but maybe he would buy a brooch or pendant.

'The prices are very reasonable, Mr. Schadel.' He began to price each item in turn but Schadel interrupted.

'The necklace! How much is the necklace?

Derek shook his head firmly. 'I am sorry, sir, but that is not for sale. Any of the other pieces, but not the necklace.'

Schadel looked at him shrewdly. 'I will buy them all for my collection,' he said finally.

It was an unexpected offer. Derek hesitated before shaking his head. 'I'm afraid the necklace is not for sale, sir. But you may buy everything else for...' And he named a price.

'All or nothing,' Schadel said sharply. 'I double your price with the necklace and I pay cash. I buy now or never!'

'Double my price!' Derek was dumb-founded. He could not resist the offer. Removing the 'Not for Sale' label, he shook hands with Karl Schadel and watched him count out the banknotes.

14

Schadel left the shop with his packet of jet jewellery and Derek, bowing politely at the door, was already wondering how he was going to handle Liz. He needed some excuse and time to find an adequate replacement for her necklace. He placed three trays of signet rings in the empty window and waited.

She noticed at once that the window display had changed. 'What's happened to the jet?' she asked, dumping shopping on the floor. The answer came in a flash.

'It all needs polishing, the surrounds were tarnished. No wonder it won't sell. I've taken them round to Jamie's...' naming a friend who dabbled in semi-precious stones. 'And by the way, he thinks some of them are French jet, made of black glass.'

'Really?' she said, putting on the kettle. 'Which ones?'

Derek said he wasn't sure, and changed the subject. Maybe he could pretend the necklace wasn't genuine jet. This was getting embarrassing, a replacement would cost quite a lot. Suddenly, with a jangle of bells, Karl Schadel entered, more lively than usual, his eyes darting round the shop mischievously.

'What do you want now, Schadel?' Derek hissed. Liz was busy in the back room.

'I wish to give a little present, in celebration of your engagement. Is your fiancée available?' And he raised his voice to attract her attention.

'What's it to do with you?' muttered Derek, terrified that Schadel would mention his purchase of the jet jewellery. 'Can't you come back some other time?'

But too late, Liz came through into the shop, smiling politely but a little warily at the unexpected visitor. She was taken aback to find Karl Schadel bowing and presenting her with a little packet.

'Why hello, Mr. Schadel,' she said. 'What's all this?'

He was smiling at her. 'Today I hear you are to marry so I offer my congratulations and a little present. Please to accept it with my sincere wishes for your future happiness.'

For a moment Liz thought he winked at her, then with eyes twinkling as he rubbed his hands together, he retreated from the

15

shop, leaving her to open the packet.

She picked up her beautiful jet necklace and knew in her heart that the old man had looked after her future happiness.

The Sussex Farmhouse Cookbook

Charles Severine was dictating a conveyancing document when the phone rang. It was his wife, his ex-wife, and considering he hadn't spoken to her for six months her request came like an unexpected court summons. She sounded rather hysterical and he had to send the secretary out of the office in case she heard too much. He had had plenty of experience of his wife's, his ex-wife's, penetrating voice, though the plaintive sobbing over the phone was unusual.

'All right, Gina, calm down,' he said. 'What's the matter?'

'I can't tell you, they might hear me,' she whimpered, suddenly lowering her voice. 'Help me, Charles, I need to talk to you.'

'Well, that's what you're doing now. How can I help?' Not for the first time, he felt obliged to respond kindly to her - some insidious form of guilt gnawing at him. He was used to the peremptory manner, which assumed his obedience, but this helplessness was different.

'Take me away from this place, Charles,' she cried.

'What, now?' he protested.

'Please! I need your help. As soon as possible.'

'Where are you?' He was checking his appointments book.

'Southease Health Farm, near Lewes. You've been before, come at once, I beg you!' And someone put down the receiver on him.

His curiosity was aroused. The final severance of their relationship had been bloody and definitive, she maintaining a frosty silence and he rejoicing in his newfound freedom. And here she was, actually pleading to see him! He had a mind to ignore the bitch, remembering the humiliations of the past, but her request was so peculiar he just had to respond. It would take him only half-an-hour to drive over to Southease and he decided to miss the Rotary Club lunch meeting, which was no hardship.

He drove through Lewes High Street, crammed with cars at midday as usual, and noticed a flower shop. It occurred to him that flowers might be acceptable, nothing romantic like roses but perhaps chrysanthemums were suitably autumnal so he pulled into a parking space nearby and chose a fine pot-plant with yellow flowers. Then, on his way back to the car he saw a second-hand bookshop further down the street, a quaint half-timbered building with walls so antique the rows of books outside seemed to act as clay and wattle. He decided to buy her a book. Inside, a hermit-like bookseller peered at him from a strategic corner.

'Do you have a cook-book section?' Charles asked, aware of the custodian's bored disapproval as a row of shelves was indicated with a dismissive wave of an arm. 'For a friend,' he added weakly, though he wasn't going to say 'For my ex-wife' even if it was true. Gina collected cookbooks. Through the stormy years of their marriage she had accumulated a library of them, gradually replacing foodstuffs in the larder until the shelves groaned under the weight of cook-books of all description, menus and recipes from all quarters of the globe, from Mrs. Beeton to the latest TV chef's gaudy publication. Not that they made her a better cook or culinary expert; it was more her way of bolstering morale as she put on weight in pursuit of exotica or experiments, as if her self-indulgence could be exonerated by a kind of academic interest in the subject. Her excesses had begun to infuriate Charles; too much wine in the casserole, too much cream on the profiteroles. He grew thinner in protest as she grew fatter. Periodically, overcome with remorse, she would practice self-denial and take herself to a Health Farm for a slim-down. But one sight of the larder of cookbooks set salivary glands secreting again.

The ancient bookshop couldn't compete with Gina's book hoard but all he was looking for was some little offering to soothe a hysterical bonne vivante cooped up on a punishing diet in a Health Farm. A hand-written card was pinned to the top shelf: Cuisines, but the random stock of cook-books included the usual leftovers and detritus of gourmets and gourmands the world over, published to titillate a million jaded palates but now remaindered and forgotten. He spotted an early Elizabeth David still in its Minton dust jacket but he wasn't spending that much on his ex-wife. He chose a 1930's publication called 'Sussex Farm-house Specialities' - because the rosy-cheeked plump farm-wife smiling on the cover reminded him of Gina in better days. He asked for a wrapping of the gift, to put beside the bouquet of chrysanthemums.

The Southease Health Farm proved to be a bit of a misnomer, being originally a tied cottage with prefab extensions linked by covered passageways. Local farms provided wholesome foodstuffs but priority seemed to be given to vitamins out of bottles, which Gina had often endured as penance for months of over-indulgence. Charles stood in front of the tacked-on portals with chrysanthemum plant and book in hand, gloomily brooding on how much he disliked the place. Parasitic, simply pandering to self-gratification and potential obesity. As a lawyer he had no time for that kind of irresponsible exploitation. Was it vanity, or some kind of personal pride, that made her so dependent on such retreats? Better to take an emetic after her feasting and sick up the excesses before the damage was done. His marriage to Gina had been a union of opposites from the start but by now they had moved so far apart she was out of sight. What was he doing here, timidly responding to his ex-wife's latest whim?

They were obviously expecting him. He was politely ushered into an office and at once a tall, white-coated doctor with a moustache that kept twitching greeted him.

'Mr. Severine, how nice to meet you. Lovely day! My name is Doctor Wellington. Well now, I know Mrs. Severine has asked you to come and see her, and before you meet her I want to explain there have been complications,' he said.

'Complications about what?

'Let me explain,' said the doctor nervously. 'Nothing to be alarmed about but I do want to warn you.'

'Warn me?'

'Mrs. Severine's rhytidectomy.'

'I beg your pardon?' He was beginning to wonder if this was some kind of joke.

'You didn't know?' said the doctor, somewhat puzzled. 'Your

wife is here convalescing after a rhytidectomy at our Clinic.'

'And what does that mean?'

'She has undergone surgery for a face-lift, Mr. Severine. The operation was conducted by Mr. Blake three days ago, one of our most reliable surgeons, but unfortunately he is er......indisposed at the present moment. Mrs. Severine had arranged to come here to convalesce after her operation. Most of our patients do this.'

'I didn't know,' said Charles, stating the obvious.

'Bear with me, sir,' replied the doctor, moustache twitching violently. 'When you meet your wife -'

'Ex-wife,' interrupted Charles.

'Ah,' commented the doctor, though it was uncertain what that meant. 'I can assure you that under the anaesthetic, the operation on Mrs. Severine's face went reasonably well. The incisions were precise and blunt scissors undermined the facial skin without risk of damage to facial mobility or paralysis. Subcutaneous fat was removed, particularly tissue along the jowl and hyoid, and the surplus skin cut off.'

'Do you mind if I sit down?' asked Charles.

'Of course not, Mr. Severine.' Charles groped for a chair and tried to settle his mind to receive more information. The doctor was stroking his moustache as if soothing it. He began walking about the room as he warmed to his subject.

'As I was saying, the stitching was normal, collagen injected properly and drainage tubes correctly inserted through incisions to guard against haematomas and -'

'What's that mean?' Charles was feeling faint.

'Haematomas is an accumulation of blood along the incision lines. I'm afraid this is where the trouble seems to have started.'

'Trouble,' said Charles dully.

'Yes, there is a failure to re-attach to the subcutaneous tissue. We had to drain --'

A nurse was entering silently, flushed and agitated, to whisper in the doctor's ear. Apparently Mrs. Severine was demanding to meet her husband without further delay, it was causing her great stress and could cause damage. Dr. Wellington became agitated and his moustache shuddered.

'Very well, thank you, nurse,' he said and turned to Charles. 'Remember, Mr. Severine, your wife will appear very different. It is always the same with face-lifts, you know.' He guided him towards the sickroom.

'Ex-wife,' muttered Charles, stumbling along the corridor.

He did not recognise her. She lay on a bed with bandages half removed from her head, as if she had been unwinding them. Her eyes glared at him, moist and bright, like stars shining through a mass of puffy clouds, the skin mottled with purple stains, her cheeks discoloured, her brow bruised and streaked. He could see the stitches behind her hairline, the skin stretched over the bone-structure. And making her look like the bride of Frankenstein's monster, drainage tubes surrounding her shrunken head.

Behind him, the doctor was hissing accusations of negligence at the nurse: she should not have left her patient alone. Charles turned on him, suddenly angry, and shouted to him to shut up and get out, to leave them on their own. The doctor threw his arms about furiously and snarled, but he reluctantly left, moustache bristling no longer. Charles looked at his ex-wife, deeply shocked, unable to speak.

'Charles, thank God!' she croaked. 'Help!' Her lips moved with difficulty. Her face had the rigidity of a mask.

'What's happened to you, Gina?' he whispered, revulsion fighting a battle with pity.

'They did this to me, the bastards!' she cried. 'It's all gone wrong. That surgeon, he had a seizure while he was operating on me, he couldn't continue, there was a delay ... they should have known, look at me, look what they've done to me! I've been bleeding for days! Such pain, you can't imagine.' Her eyes glittered and her voice suddenly grated. 'Sue them, Charles, I want you to sue them!'

Tears filled her eyes and leaked down her cheeks, her mouth bubbled with saliva, her prostrate flabby body shook with anguish or rage. The nurse was busy patting her brow, intent on stopping her move, glancing at him impatiently as if he was to blame.

'She'll be all right, give it time,' said the nurse.

He wondered if anyone could recover from such a trauma, even if her flesh were to heal. A wave of sympathy for Gina, victim of an operation that had gone wrong, swept through him but there was part of him that resented his own involvement. He had not known what was going on, no one had informed him. No wonder she had sent for him; she wanted his legal expertise even though she was his ex-wife. A face-lift! What had that to do with him? And she won't pay me, he thought, I don't even know what she signed up for or the terms of the contract. But he could hardly walk out and wash his hands of her.

'Yes of course,' he said soothingly, aware that her left eyelid was quivering neurotically. He had to sit down and, still holding the pot of chrysanthemums and the gift book, he perched on the side of the bed and then had to apologise as Gina's leg, trapped under his weight, was hurriedly removed from its position. He looked round for a chair but the only one was against the wall and the nurse was obviously unwilling to help. He got up to walk across the room and realised that his pair of hands were holding the flowerpot and the book. Suddenly he thrust the flowers in front of her so she could see the bold autumnal colours. The musty aroma from the flowers momentarily blended with sharp anaesthetic odours. Standing there, waiting for her to react, he felt grotesque and tactless. What good were flowers at a time like this? Gina seemed unimpressed. Looking at the flowers, she growled and flapped a hand at him angrily, knocking the pot out of his extended hand. Soil spilled on to the sheet before the nurse was able to retrieve the pot-plant. With an irritated sidelong glance at Severine, she placed the chrysanthemums on the side-table and left to fetch a brush and pan. He felt he was having to take the blame for the upset and felt annoyed.

'Sue them!' Gina spat venomously.

'All right, all right, I will,' he assured her. Then he remembered he had something else to give her.

'I thought you might like this for your cook-book collection, Gina. I got it at the local bookshop,' he added unnecessarily.

He held out the cookery book so she could see the title: 'Sussex Farmhouse Specialities' and the illustration on the cover. Perhaps she would like this little present at least.

Gina gazed at the book, raised her eyes to study him and great waves of emotion shuddered through her. Silently at first, then with increasing wails and sobs she broke into a lament that continued for some minutes, her body shaking with anguish, tears running down her puffed cheeks, mouth agape to allow the grief to pour out in moans.

For a while he stood bewildered, uncertain why the book should cause this emotional outburst, then without comprehending what he was doing, he dropped the book on the floor and knelt by her side as she lay with mutilated head on the pillow, cradling her overweight frame that wobbled and shook uncontrollably as she wept in a confusion of self-pity, pain, regret and venom.

He felt trapped. She was his ex-wife, he no longer loved her, he wanted no part of her, the hideous spectacle of her wrecked body repulsed him but he was still holding her in his arms, muttering tenderly, when the nurse returned to clean up the bed linen.

Heads or Tails

As a teenager my Aunt Edna screamed at the Beatles, smoked pot, danced topless at Glastonbury and meditated transcendentally with a Cockney guru, which for a respectable Scotswoman is, to say the least, unusual. When Poppy and I were infants, not so long ago really, she would lull us to sleep by gently crooning 'Ground Control to Major Tom' or 'Eleanor Rigby', and recount vivid memories of the fab days instead of fairy tales and lullabies. Poppy is Aunt Edna's daughter. When my parents split up, I stayed for a few months with my Aunt and jolly nice it was too, with Poppy as a constant companion. I suppose I've been in love with her ever since.

Forty years on, Aunt Edna's flower power is on the wane, but she is still my favourite Aunt. For one thing, through all my adolescent period of growing up, she never criticised me for being a bit of a geek. And for another, I knew she would always tell me the latest news of Poppy and her adventures. From a distance though. Poppy is one of those girls who can see more on the horizon than you could possibly imagine, starting with skate-boarding and before you've picked yourself off the ground she's into para-gliding or caving. Poppy always looks good in a helmet with her blonde curls bursting round. Taking a year out to explore the Brazilian rain-forests was no surprise, nor was getting her glider-pilot certificate. I never actually stood at the end of a railway platform collecting train numbers but Poppy made me feel something like an anorak. She has never called me that but she has to laugh when I look at her with the eyes of a King Charles spaniel. Once she called me a wet-nosed nerd but she was hugging me at the time and it was only fun so I wasn't offended, it showed she cares for me one way or another. I gave up following her around years ago but I keep up with all the news from Aunt Edna. Just now Poppy is at Brands Hatch testing Formula One racing cars; she's in some kind of syndicate aiming to take over the English Grand Prix and apparently she's always tinkering with internal combustion engines. She's definitely supercharged herself.

Getting a letter or a phone call from Poppy is just about as rare as a telegram from the Queen, so you can imagine my astonishment to find an e-mail from her one evening when I get back from the office. I had to read it five times before I got the gist: *'Hi Robin. Dad's bust a gasket. Please head for good old s by the s. Stiff upper lip. Poppy'*. Of course I got on the blower at once, asking certain members of the family if they knew anything. It seems Poppy's father, Uncle Ernest, has died rather unexpectedly while out on the local golf links. He had a dicky heart, which is why he and Aunt Edna retired early to Bexhill-on-Sea, but when he sank a twenty yard putt on the thirteenth green he dropped dead either from shock or delight, which may be a good way to go but is somewhat traumatic for those left behind, in particular poor Aunt Edna with her flower-power growing weedy. Reading the sub-text of Poppy's e-mail, I construed a theory that there was a bit more to this sad event than a bereavement. I drop everything and next day head for the south coast. Poppy needs me!

There's an Alfa-Romeo sports car outside the bungalow when I arrive, and it looks as if someone has tried but failed to close the curtains, which are looking sadly dishevelled. When I ring the bell a strange woman opens the door and welcomes me. She's a neighbour and whispers condolences as she ushers me into the front room. I can see Aunt Edna sitting in an armchair, dabbing her eyes with a handkerchief and looking mournful and depressed. Beside her sits a man who leans forward, pats her hand and seems totally absorbed in attending her.

'Robin!' cries Aunt Edna, and flaps her hankie at me.

'Don't get up, my dear!' the man says and turns to face me. He's bony and angular with a wide smile as if skin won't stretch far enough to shut his mouth. His teeth are too regular to be natural. His hair, which even I can see is dyed, is combed straight back and glistens in furrows. He moves forward, arm extended, to greet me with a vigorous handshake.

'So this is Robin! Hello, heard a lot about you, young man. Pleased to meet you. Don't stand on ceremony eh, we're all retiring types around here ha ha. Norman's the name, Squadron Leader Norman Fowles, next door neighbour.'

He is wearing a blazer with brass buttons and an RAF crest on the top pocket. He seems to have very long legs or perhaps unusually tight trouser-legs. Standing centrally he blocks any sight of Aunt Edna, whom I am waiting to meet.

'I was with Ernest on the golf course, you know,' said Norman Fowles, leaning forward conspiratorially. 'Totally unexpected, I was amazed, especially at the thirteenth hole, quite remarkable.'

'His death?' I said, a little uncertain what was so amazing.

He guffawed. 'No no, I mean his twenty yard putt! Ernest wasn't that good, you know! But in it went, straight as a laser, down in one. Poor old Ernest, took him by surprise, he went down in one too. Tragic business! A bit of a bind for me at the time.'

We were interrupted by Aunt Edna, unable to wait any longer to embrace me. Moving across to claim me, she cried, 'Robin darling! How nice to see you!' and we fell into each other's arms. I held her close, my favourite Aunt, grieving for her loss but not able to say anything that might adequately express my deep love for her. Norman stands back, rubbing his hands and nodding his head as he runs through a whole gamut of empty consolations, accompanied by little chuckles.

'Terrible loss ha ha, absolutely devastating ha ha, heartfelt sympathies ha, a real pukka type, you know, splendid character ha ha, time will tell, rest in peace.'

I feel like kicking the clumsy oaf when I suffer a sudden pain in the small of the back. I know at once what is causing it, I can recognize that sharp jabbing action anywhere, and I turn to face Poppy, who is now glaring at me furiously, her face screwed up with some kind of intense distaste.

'Poppy!' I cry, glad both to see her and to turn my back on this insufferable stranger who takes Aunt Edna's arm and leads her back to her chair.

'Robin, you prat! What took you so long?' asks Poppy after we have hugged each other.

'I haven't got an Alfa-Romeo, you know!' I reply, quite wittily I thought.

'Oh that!' she says offhandedly. 'It belongs to my boyfriend.' I don't know why she tells me that, it's not as if I'm the jealous type, but I can see she's upset and has been crying and I squeeze her hand daringly.

'Sorry about your Dad, Poppy old thing,' I say. 'Everything okay?' I am aware of lower lips quivering but before we can say any more, Norman makes a public announcement.

'Time for a cuppa! All ranks fall in for the cup that cheers! Are you receiving me, Mrs. Dent?' This to the other neighbour, who very attentively is acting as the char-lady for she immediately departs to the kitchen. It seems as if this Squadron Leader character has taken over the running of our domestic airfield; even now he is plumping a cushion and fussily placing it behind Aunt Edna's head. She looks very tired, grateful for his attention but still withdrawn. Her eyebrows, which always arched so wonderingly, seem to have fallen with bewilderment. She must be suffering from shock and could probably do with a quiet rest, but there wasn't much chance of that with Norman Fowles swooping over her like a Junkers dive-bomber.

'See you outside!' hisses Poppy in my ear and disappears through the door, leaving me to browse round the room looking at pictures on the wall. Most of them I know well: family groups, one with me smiling as Aunt Edna's arms encircle my head and Poppy sits on her Dad's knee. A view of Venice from a gondola. Poppy in a Spitfire. Students grouped round a big carved stone, somewhere on the Inca trail. A young Aunt Edna with someone who looks like Mick Jagger in a kilt. And then, on a side-table, a new head and shoulder photograph, airbrushed for glamour, of Norman Fowles smirking at the camera. He's even signed the damned thing: 'To dear Edna and Ernest with Love from Norman.' I glance across at him as he gently pats the hand of my Aunt who murmurs to herself; he caws soothingly like a great gaunt crow. Time to answer Poppy's call.

'Sorry,' I blurt, 'Need the loo, won't be long.' Neither of them appears to care very much; Aunt Edna nods rather miserably and the Squadron Leader shows his teeth amicably. Quickly I leave the room and Poppy is obviously furious having to wait so long for me,

28

for she's beckoning me to come outside the front door where we can talk quietly. I can see she's in one of her glorious rages. I love her when the adrenalin flows and a halo glows round her head. She's Joan of Arc without the armour or the voices for that matter, and she makes me feel like the Dauphin.

'That bloody long streak of piss!' she mutters as we stand on the doorstep. Poppy does not often resort to verbal abuse but when she does, she means it. Maybe acquaintance with big ends and carburettors was widening her vocabulary, I could almost smell the engine oil.

'Er – you mean Norman?

'He's after her!'

'Er – you mean Aunt Edna?'

'Who d'you think, pinhead!'

'Yes of course.'

'The absolute bastard!'

'Norman?'

I received a confirming thump on my arm. Poppy's eyes gleamed with fury.

'Grow up, you thicko, can't you see? He's after my Mum!'

'Ah,' I agreed. 'He does seem to be dancing attendance on her.'

'Don't be funny, Robin. This is serious. He's got some kind of hold on her.'

'How long has this been going on?'

'He moved in a year ago, next door neighbour. Dad liked him, for some reason, they played golf together, and both liked a flutter.'

'Flutter?'

'Gambling! They dabbled on the gee-gees. And stocks and shares. Mum put up with it, I know she didn't like him but Dad did. It's because he has that Queen Anne silver crown.'

'What?' Poppy suddenly seemed to be losing her thread.

'He's a bloody numismatist!'

I must admit my geographic expertise is not up to scratch. I ask Poppy if that meant Norman Fowles was a political refugee.

Normally she would have keeled over with laughter at my ignorance but this time she started shaking me with rage. I quite enjoyed it actually, like being manhandled by a muscular angel.

That's when the Squadron Leader stuck his head round the door. He assumed there was some kind of hanky panky going on between Poppy and me. Winking and braying, he informed us that tea and cucumber sandwiches were ready. Together we re-entered the bungalow, with Poppy trying to control her emotions and me relishing every bruise and buffet. After the tea and sandwiches, courtesy of Mrs. Dent, we both stayed to comfort Aunt Edna though that wasn't easy with Norman butting in at every possible moment. At last, he seemed to realise he couldn't hang around all day and got up to go. He suddenly pulled a shining disc from his pockets and called, 'Heads for another cuppa! Tails, it's time to get back to base!' Flicking the coin in the air, he caught and upturned it on his hand.

Peering at it, he shook his head sadly. 'Tails it is! Queen Anne knows what's what. Got to get cracking, orders from her majesty, ha ha!'

Poppy was digging me in the ribs. 'That's his silver crown!' she hissed. None the wiser, I watched as he went round the room shaking hands and showing everyone this unusual coin, bigger than any modern currency and obviously a relic of the past.

'My best friend is Queen Anne!' he chortled. 'She knows the drill: don't overstay your welcome. Thank you, ma'am!' He was pocketing the coin wrapped in a small black velvet purse. He shook my hand enthusiastically but his smile was ingratiating.

'Ah,' I said rather feebly. 'I hear you collect coins. You are a munismatist!'

I was rather offended by his response to my slip. He more or less fell about laughing. I mean, tongue-twisters have always tied me in knots and anyone could have made a mistake over that word. There was certainly no reason to be sarcastic.

'**Num**ismatist, old man! It's a very long word but can you spell it? Not I – Tee ! En you em I ess em ay tee I es tee! Tell you what, next time you're down, come and take a blick at my collection. Worth seeing eh, Poppy?'

She didn't reply but waited for him to leave, aware that I had made a bit of a fool of myself. He was kissing Aunt Edna's hand and murmuring endearments. Then he left, passing through a small gate in the fence that separated their bungalows. Poppy and I decided to retreat to the local pub, leaving Aunt Edna to rest, and at last we were on our own.

2

The funeral took place ten days after that visit to Bexhill-on-Sea, a family occasion with appropriate dignity and a eulogy on Uncle Ernest spoken by a doddery octogenarian who remembered him as a little boy. He seemed quite pleased to be twenty years older than the deceased. 'We who are left behind...' he said at least twice with evident satisfaction. Aunt Edna became very tearful as he went on reviving memories. She always said it was Ernest who had saved her from a roadie's life and their marriage was happy though he had been a bit of a gambler in his time. Poppy told me that was why he had got on so well with Norman. They would spend hours just spinning coins and calling 'heads' or 'tails' until one of them ran out of pocket money. She said it was rather like watching Rosencrantz and Guildenstern in that play about Hamlet, but Aunt Edna had got a bit worried when they started speculating on the stock exchange and seemed to be tossing coins to decide whether to buy or sell shares. Another thing the octogenarian said about Ernest's forays in the City - he was more of a bull than a bear, which made a few of the mourners at the cremation service titter but I was a bit confused and wondered if that was supposed to mean Norman was a bear rather than a bull. I glanced across at Poppy sitting by her mother but she wasn't smiling.

We hadn't had much chance to talk since arriving at the crematorium and there was plenty to ask about, including how Aunt Edna was coping with Norman. Poor Aunt was looking quite frail in a beautifully old way but the trouble was, she needed some kind of moral support now she was on her own, and he was always on hand, sliding through that little gate between the two bungalows with bunches of tulips or boxes of chocolates. I couldn't be sure how much she liked Norman but she certainly couldn't reject his advances, for apparently he behaved impeccably whenever he was with her. In fact, as Poppy drove back to the bungalow with me as her nervous passenger, I talked to her like a Dutch Uncle, trying to cool her explosive vehemence.

'Hang on a bit, Poppy, maybe your Mum doesn't mind him.'

'Mind him!' Poppy positively screamed at me. 'How can she stand that hypocritical, oily worm? I hate him!'

'It takes all sorts, old girl. Steady on round this bend, you don't know anything about him.'

'I've seen enough,' she retorted, swinging round a curve. 'I don't trust him. He's always playing tricks on her with his coins, especially that heads or tails game. You know what he's after, don't you? Mum's money.'

'Poppy, that's bunk. He wants to be friends, that's all!'

'He's proposed.'

'What? Marriage?'

'On his knees, crawling all round her, kissing her hand, slobbering.'

'You heard him?'

'Seeing was enough. I fled from the disgusting scene.'

'You're exaggerating,' I protested, as the Alfa-Romeo howled along the lanes. I decided to say no more, just in case she stamped her foot in rage.

And sure enough, back at the bungalow for the funeral wake, as we sipped our drinks and nibbled sweetmeats, Norman was fussing around Aunt Edna, sharing with her the role of host and hostess, offering a wee dram of whisky to all and sundry, cracking jokes that seemed to go down well and wanting to tell fortunes from tea leaves in cups. He was obviously well practised at entertaining people in the parlour. He took a number of coins from his pockets and invited people to play 'Spot the Lady' with him, laying three coins on the table and covering them with teacups. Time and again people pointed to the wrong teacup and Norman made great play of slyly revealing the right coin. All three coins looked pretty antique but the real lady was heads up and showed the profile of a queen from the past no doubt. I don't know how he did it, but his long bony fingers were constantly gyrating over the cups and this deceptive legerdemain kept the audience guessing and bursting into flurries of laughter. Aunt Edna looked on graciously, perhaps grateful that Norman was able to put all the guests at their ease, except for Poppy and me, who stood in a corner of the room observing all this jollity with dismay. Poppy was absolutely the ghost at the feast and I felt pretty ghoulish myself, though I have to admit if it were not for her I might have enjoyed Norman's conjuring tricks.

Eventually the guests started to depart, and I could see Aunt Edna was relieved to come to the end of this 'wake'. Poppy was going round the room collecting plates, cups and saucers to take to the kitchen when suddenly I saw Norman bearing down on me, a rapacious smirk on his face. He held my arm in a firm grip, clearly determined to have his way.

'Well, old boy,' he chortled, 'it's chocks away. Jolly good show, wizard seeing you again. Tell you what, care for a rekky over at my place? Got a thing or two to show you.'

I looked round for Poppy, in desperation. She was absorbed in reaching the kitchen sink with a tray full of teetering crockery. I was on my own.

'Ah righty-ho,' I gulped.

'Roger and out!' he jargoned at me and led the way, out of the front door and through the side gate into his garden. Tulips of many colours stood to attention in stiff rows bordering the bungalow, which looked very similar to Aunt Edna's. The lawn was smooth enough for snooker. A kind of Muscovy hound suddenly appeared, wagging its tail, yapping and demanding recognition as guardian, and Norman fondled it while I weighed up its potential for violence.

'Good boy, who's a lovely boy! All right, it's only me, calm down,' Norman cried soothingly. 'This is Robin, Edna's favourite nephew ha ha. His name's Winston. Make friends, Robin, there's a good dog!'

Winston's cold wet nose and spongy tongue had already soaked my hand. Feebly I patted him, trying to wipe off saliva on his fur, and was relieved when Norman ushered me into the bungalow. The first thing that struck me about the open-plan living room was the clutter of ashtrays and ornaments that seemed to be memorabilia of war service in the RAF and aircraft of all kinds. There were four model aircraft suspended from the ceiling, one of which I recognized as a Tiger Moth. And an extraordinary number of photographs of groups of pilots gathered round Spitfires and Hurricanes hanging on the walls. Could these all relate to squadrons that he had led or commanded? I began to wonder if this geezer was some kind of anorak himself. He led me along a corridor where two crossed propellers stuck out far enough to obstruct the passageway. There was a solid-looking door with a padlock beyond those shining blades and Norman approached it with a smirk. He waved a large key at me, winked and said, 'This, Robin, is the key to Fort Knox!'

He opened the door, and I called out 'Knox, knox, who's there?' which I thought was just about up to speed for witty quick thinking until Norman switched the lights on. I realised I should have said, 'Open sesame!' for it was Aladdin's Cave in there, all lit up with concealed lighting, shining coins displayed like stars and constellations twinkling in rows. There were drawers, boxes, cabinets and shelves cunningly spot lit, with neat little cards beside each exhibit.

'Golly!' I exclaimed. 'You really are a numismatist!' and this time I got it right.

Norman began to describe the treasures of his collection, handling one coin after another as if they were precious gems. He seemed to know an awful lot about coins and he definitely had a mighty haul of them to chunter on about. Now I don't know about you but I've never been much of a collector. A few years back I used to pinch beer-mats out of pubs where me and my mates drank and they looked okay on the wall, lined up like – well, like beer-mats really, but Poppy said they were useless up there so I took them down. I was thinking that was a bit like Norman's coin collection actually, because they were not legal tender so that makes them pretty useless too, until he started to tell me how much some of the coins were worth. I was gobsmacked to learn the contents of that room could fetch thousands of pounds at auctions but that didn't mean I wanted a five-hour lecture on numismatics. My eyes were beginning to glaze and I was stifling yawns when there was a change of tone in Norman's voice, no longer a dreary string of long-winded sentences but much more urgent and confidential.

He had produced the black velvet purse, which I recognized from the game of 'Spot the Lady' in Aunt Edna's sitting room, and now he laid the silver coin on the table, where it glittered under the spotlights. 'This coin,' he said, 'is worth a couple of thousand but I value it for other reasons. This is very special. It is helping me to win the hand of the lady I love.'

I sat up sharply. He was no longer talking about coins, but Aunt Edna.

'I am very fond of your dear Aunt,' he confided. 'I should be extremely chuffed if she accepts my hand in marriage. I'm not shooting a line, I'm the right type for her. I can look after her. Trouble is her daughter takes a dim view of me, she is completely cheesed off about me. I need your help, Robin.'

Suddenly I was in an embarrassing situation – this man was used to giving orders and yet here he was pleading for help with a long face, droopy mouth and sad eyes that reminded me of a white-faced clown. I looked for the teardrop in the corner of his eye but there was none. Didn't he realise whose side I was on? And what had all this to do with the coin?

'You see this coin?' he asked, as if reading my mind. 'It's a silver crown from the reign of Queen Anne, dated 1707. The obverse shows her profile. See?'

I leaned forward to study the head on the coin. She's looking to the left, her hair neatly arranged over her head, middle-aged and with a double chin. Rather plum duff actually. And round her profile are the words ANNA DEI GRATIA, which I think translate as 'Anne thanks to God'. I'm scratching my head to remember my English history lessons, trying to fit Queen Anne somewhere between William and Mary and George the first, when Norman turns the coin over.

'Do you know what happened in 1707, Robin?' he said.

I thought that was a silly question. All kinds of things happen every year. I studied the coin looking for clues. There were four little shields separated by a cross. I suddenly had an inspiration.

'Queen Anne died,' I guessed.

'No, those shields bear the arms of England and Scotland. In 1707 England and Scotland became united as one nation!' cried Norman, an excited gleam in his eyes. 'This coin commemorates the event and I'm hoping it will commemorate another union - between Edna who is Scottish and Norman who is English! There's magic in it, you see.'

I didn't exactly giggle but I couldn't stop thinking this chap was obviously a nutcase. Maybe I should humour him.

'Oh really? And how does it work, this magic?'

'I'm not sure,' he replied, taking me very seriously, 'but Ernest knew all about it.'

'Uncle Ernest?'

'Yes. We used to speculate on the Stock Exchange and if we weren't certain, we would spin the coin. I don't know how it started but we got used to saying, 'Salve, Anna dei Gratia' and asked her to advise us. If she came down head up, that meant 'yes' and we'd invest or sell shares Sometimes she said 'no' and that's when the reverse side is tail up. Not just money matters, other things, like Ernest's new car, she advised him 'not to buy'.'

'Just as well, considering, ' I said.

'It's funny but she always gives good advice.'

'Does Aunt Edna know about this?'

'Of course. She's got a theory about thought transference, and ions and electrons being affected by positive thinking. Darling Edna! Very New Worldy. It's why I find her so adorable.'

'So, let me guess,' I responded impertinently. 'You want her to toss this silver crown to decide whether she should accept your proposal of marriage.'

He nodded his head gravely. 'This is no joke, Robin. I am desperate. It's my best chance of persuading her to marry me. At the moment she won't budge. Edna will not agree to marry me unless Poppy agrees. I am willing to trust fate as directed by Queen Anne. This coin has succeeded so many times, I shall hope for her support. If I fail, well, I shall be in the drink, shot down in flames.'

'And me, how do I help?'

'You try to get Poppy to agree. After all, the Queen may not be on my side.'

'But it's nonsense!' I exclaimed. 'You can't believe in it, any more than I do!'

He looked at me directly, as if to prove his honesty. 'I know only that it works well enough for me to hope.'

'Let me see that coin,' I demanded. Biting it hard, tasting it, smelling it, dropping it, spinning it - I could find no flaws in the metal or signs of magic trickery. The whole proposition was ridiculous, of course, but I had to admire the way he was handling the situation. Asking for the Queen's advice had been an accepted part of their decision-making for some time. If it was on the level it wasn't a bad idea to take the gamble, from Norman's point of view. It would all be pretty straightforward - you asked the question: the coin was spun and could come down heads or tails.

I could see what my job would be - keep my eyes skinned, my ears pricked, my suspicions well primed to ensure no double-crossing took place. And now it was getting a bit claustrophobic in Aladdin's Cave and I needed fresh air. Thanking Squadron Leader Norman Fowles for showing me his remarkable collection of coins, I returned to Aunt Edna's bungalow. Poppy of course was hopping mad at me, not really knowing where I had been, but the washing up was done and Aunt Edna was putting things away and sweetly crooning one of her nostalgic ballads. It was lovely to see mother and daughter enjoying each other so much. Poppy, for all her restless impetuosity, was gentle and loving at heart. Aunt Edna put on a cheerful front, sitting quietly and recalling happy moments with Ernest. I decided to say nothing about Norman's stratagem with the Queen Anne silver crown, for I didn't want to spoil their domestic contentment. Poppy sent me away with a flea in my ear, for she couldn't understand how I could spend so long with that poisonous insect next door, and when I glanced round to wave goodbye, I could see they were very content to be left on their own.

3

Well, you know how it is. As soon as you're back in the smoke it's the usual routine, down the health club two or three times a week, do a work-out, sweat and take a shower, get beaten at squash again (tiddlywinks is more my style), jog a bit (walk mainly), relax in 'the Swan', meet the guys, drink too much, cool it with a video back at the flat, and oh yeah, suss out that book group, and all on top of thirty hours shift work at the office. It's a mug's game up here, I really ought to consider a quiet life in the country. No wonder I don't keep in touch.

I phoned Aunt Edna a few times, always glad to hear that brogue (more Edinburgh than Glasgow) spoken so musically and she seemed very relaxed. I asked if she is lonely.

'Och, not at all,' she replied lightly, 'dinna fash yourself. There's plenty to do in Bexhill for the likes of me. I take a wee walk every day, with Winston at times.'

'Who?'

'Winston, Norman's dog.'

'Ah yes, Winston. How is he?' I was asking about Norman actually.

'A bit of distemper, but the vet cleared that up. How's yourself?'

It took some time to describe the minor ailments that were at that time afflicting me. Aunt Edna may have got a bit bored for she put the phone down on me. As for Poppy, I lost touch with her completely. It was more difficult than usual to get her to stand still and pick up her mobile. She was over in Le Mans, in hot pursuit of some darkly handsome driver I didn't like the sound of at all, so I let slip any chance to tell her about Norman's plan to use the Queen

Anne silver crown. In fact I was beginning to forget all about it, that is, until I got this phone call on my landline. She's in the pits at Le Mans; someone is revving up an engine in French; it sounds like a Jumbo jet and she has to shout.

'Hi Robby, okay? A quickie! Can you make it to Mum's this weekend?'

'I suppose so. What's up?'

'Trouble down at t'mill, something to do with Queen Anne.'

'Ah, right, I was meaning to tell you – '

'Sorry! Can't say more right now. See you Saturday. Cheers!'

There's a chorus of banshees seeing her off and then the line goes dead. What can I do but wait till I get down to Bexhill-on-Sea?

The first thing I notice is that there's a small Renault outside the bungalow. Aunt Edna opens the door, smiling and embracing me warmly, quite her old self, you might say. She is expecting me because I have left a message on her answer phone, and she's so pleased because this is going to be a special weekend. I ask if Poppy has arrived.

'Och aye,' she replies, 'she came earlier.' And Aunt Edna button-holes me to whisper, 'Poor Poppy's no longer got the Alfa-Romeo, that's all over. He was married anyway. Don't say anything, she's very upset.'

Indeed, she is. She looks run down, swollen eyes betraying her smile as she greets me. Her hair is glorious as ever but unkempt, and I can't avoid the whiff of petrol underlying the perfume she's dabbed on. I can't stifle my concern.

'Poppy, what's up with you, darling?' I gasp, wanting to take her in my arms but not daring to in case she reacts badly.

'It's all right, Robin,' she says. 'I'll get over it. It's just that I have been a bit of a fool. It won't be the first time.' She's smiling a trifle ruefully. Maybe, when the time is ripe, she'll tell me more about this mishap so I don't pursue my enquiries.

'Your Mum looks well,' I say, which is true but it makes Poppy suddenly advance on me.

'Don't say that! They are engaged!' she hisses.

'What?' I gawp at her.

'Engaged to be married.'

'No!'

'Yes!'

'How did it happen?'

'He's been pestering her. And playing tricks.'

'What do you mean?'

'I don't know. Giving her presents, taking her out to dinner, playing that game with her.'

'What game?'

'Heads or tails. Queen Anne, whether she comes down heads or tails. They have been asking her to decide. He offered to sell his bungalow and move in with Mum, and Queen Anne came down tails. Then he asked if they could get engaged. It came down heads. And d'you know what? He said it was a message from Ernest on the other side, it showed he was blessing their engagement.'

'That's not fair,' I protested. 'Emotional blackmail!'

'But it worked. Mum told me it could be true. She feels Dad is trying to help her.'

'Uncle Ernest would never be so stupid,' I said. 'It's outrageous!'

Poppy was suddenly reviving, her body more erect, a halo round her head, her voice strong and vituperative.

'We have to do something *now*, Robin!'

'Whatever you command,' I say, stiffening my shoulders courageously.

'Right!' she says. 'Kill Norman!'

'He's already dead!' I reply. I feel Poppy's kiss upon my lips. Something tells me we are acting in some kind of drama. I struggle to get back to earth.

'Wait a minute, Poppy,' I demur. 'You don't want him really dead, do you? What does your Mum think about all this?'

'I know what she thinks!' cries Poppy. 'She thinks this evening Norman Fowles will be calling round with his silver crown and he'll be asking Queen Anne to say whether my Mum should marry him. And we've got to stop him!' Her voice suddenly flutes up an octave, panic being not far away. Clearly Poppy is very upset and I try to comfort her.

Aunt Edna calls 'Tea, children!'and trips into the room bearing a tray replete with refreshments. Nothing like afternoon tea in Bexhill to settle a nervous disposition. I notice she is wearing a sparkling engagement ring as she hands out the cups of tea and Aunt goes all shy, rather like a schoolgirl admitting a crush. Norman has been so kind and helpful, he really is charming and she doesn't want to disappoint him too much. She looks so sadly at her daughter as she speaks, I can't help thinking maybe they could be happy together and, if only Poppy would stop being so jealous, there could be a future for this relationship.

Poppy is in no mood for reconciliation, though. She rises and leaves the room, telling us she wants to be alone and she is going for a walk. After she has gone, Aunt Edna sighs and wistfully wishes her daughter was not so headstrong and critical of other people. Then she begins to grow quite angry. She claims Poppy doesn't realise what it is like living on her own in Bexhill, and she dabs her eyes with a handkerchief. I mumble commiserations; aware that in one hour's time Norman is due to make his fateful visit to his beloved Edna.

4

The clock strikes six, and still no sign of Poppy. Aunt Edna nervously re-arranges the flowers and prepares bowls of nuts and crisps. There's not a lot I can do, except keep out of her way. At the back of the fridge I can see a champagne bottle, what's that for? It might have been there some time. I am in the kitchen, eating olives and spitting out the stones three feet from the sink when the back door bursts opens and Poppy is standing there, glowing with excitement and hushing me in case her mother hears what she is saying. The radiance is shining all round her, making me feel weak at the knees. Mischief gleams in her eyes as she comes to me, smiling demonically. This is more like the Poppy I know and love.

'I've fixed him,' she whispers. 'I took Winston for a walk and let him off the leash on the beach. He'll be out looking for his dog for hours.'

'Didn't Norman see you?'

'Course not, I waited till he went inside.'

'Where is he now?'

'Looking for Winston, I hope.'

'He won't be coming here then. Brilliant!' Impulsively I lean forward to kiss her flushed cheek and nearly fall over, for there is a sudden ring of the front door bell and Norman's wheedling voice announces his arrival. Poppy and I freeze. Norman hasn't missed the dog. We listen as Aunt Edna greets him and they go into the sitting room.

'What do we do now?' asks Poppy hoarsely.

'What can we do?' I reply.

'Think of something, quick!' she cries, pummelling me for some sign of action.

'We go through with it,' I say. 'Trust to Queen Anne.'

'Are you mad? What good will that do?'

'It's up to your Mum. All she has to say is 'no'.'

'But will she?'

'You can't force her, Poppy.'

'I could murder him.'

I try to calm her. 'No you couldn't. We have to keep cool, play the game, make sure he doesn't cheat. Listen, Poppy, she's your mother but you don't live with her any more. She can do what she likes.' And then I say something I wouldn't ordinarily dare to. 'Grow up, girl!' I say.

Listen to me! I'm talking to my heroine as if we're equals. I'm giving her advice and instead of slagging me off, she's quietly crying, clinging to me, taking it all in. I tell her she has to control herself, try to behave normally, support her mother. Poppy nods

42

dumbly, composes herself and we enter the living room, where Aunt Edna and Norman are sipping wine. It's all polite conversation for a while, with both of us dreading the moment when Norman will start to put his cards on the table. And now he is fumbling in his blazer pocket and pulling out the familiar black velvet purse. Aunt Edna is smiling at him and nodding, not exactly encouraging him but allowing him to indulge his little whim. The moment has come. He extracts the silver coin and lays it on the table, Queen Anne's profile uppermost. He rubs his hands together, presses his fingers as if about to pray and sits quietly waiting.

'I want to inspect that coin!' cries Poppy abruptly. 'I expect it's double-headed.'

'Poppy, don't be rude,' says Aunt Edna gently. 'Norman would never do that.'

Norman smirks and flaps his hands expansively. 'By all means inspect it, my dear Poppy, I think you will find it genuine enough.'

Poppy picks up the coin and tests it aggressively. She shows it to me. Definitely this is the same Queen Anne silver crown I examined in Aladdin's Cave, with the shields on one side and the profile on the obverse. I hand it back to him and watch as he starts to conduct some kind of finger ceremony over the coin on the table, as if deliberately trying to provoke a response, which Poppy soon provides when she sits up and shouts, 'Stop messing about and get on with it, you bloody idiot!'

Aunt Edna immediately protests. 'Poppy, there's no need for bad language!' and Norman bridles at Poppy's words. 'Idiot, am I?' he says. 'You mind what you're saying, young lady. A little more respect, if you please.'

Poppy sneers, I placate, Aunt Edna apologises while Norman puts Queen Anne back in the velvet purse on the table. Then he folds his arms over it and tells us we're not ready to go on.

'We need to create a more intimate ambience. Robin, close the curtains please. And let's put the reading lamp on the table.'

While he fusses around adjusting the light, I am out of my seat closing the curtains. The room suddenly becomes mysteriously darker except over the table. I try to keep an eye on the black purse, not trusting him an inch. It is still there and as soon as I sit down again he extracts the silver crown and lays it on the table, where it catches the light. I have a sudden thought: how is he going to play this game? Does he catch the coin and turn it upside down on the other hand?

When I ask, Poppy bounces up, 'Cheat! You can turn it over to suit yourself!'

Norman looks aggrieved and just a little smug. 'My dear Poppy, let nature take its course. I won't touch it. We will ask your mother to spin the coin and let it fall on the table. Perhaps we can try again, now,' he says, a trifle sarcastically. Poppy sits glowering but silent as Norman repeats his elaborate rigmarole, with long fingers weaving a spell over the coin on the table. Drawing a deep breath, he speaks.

'Salve, Anna dei Gratia!' he says in matter-of-fact tones with no attempt to indulge in colourful oratory. And after a moment of silence he asks quietly: 'Do you bless our union in holy matrimony?'

Full marks to Norman Fowles so far, I am thinking. He's got his special effects and his intimate ambience and the audience is gripped, waiting for the action. He hands the coin to Aunt Edna and she, hands quivering with nerves, balances the silver crown on forefinger and thumb, ready for the fateful flick that will send it spinning in a curve. She looks at Poppy, then me and last, with a tensing of her arms, at Norman.

'Spin it high, my dear,' he urges, and she flicks her thumb firmly under the coin. It spins upward and then arches to descend, striking the table loudly and, before anyone can stop it, bouncing off and dropping to the floor. Norman's leg suddenly lunges forward and his foot stamps down on it. We know it's there but can't see which side is up. Aunt Edna has her head in her hands, her eyes closed. Poppy is on her knees jerking at Norman's leg, shouting at him to move his shoe. I am transfixed, staring at Norman, wondering if this has been planned. Unmoved, Norman calls for order and I reach across to hold back Poppy who is still furious and capable of launching an assault.

44

'Keep back!' yells Norman. 'Don't spoil it. Sit down, Poppy!' I sit by Poppy, calming her. He asks Aunt Edna if she is all right and she nods. Then Norman lifts his foot and exposes the coin. It is obverse side up. We stare down at it, uncertain what happens next. Queen Anne looks impassive but judgemental. Norman stoops to pick up the coin. Carefully he places it on the table and smiles at Aunt Edna. 'Queen Anne blesses our union, my dear! Congratulations!' he says, and slips the silver crown into the black velvet purse and pockets it.

Now this is where it gets tricky. Alarm bells ring in my head. Why is he so keen to put Queen Anne back to bed? I stand up at once and challenge him. I want to look at that black velvet purse. Smiling indulgently, he fishes in his pocket and produces it, but when Poppy takes the coin out, she finds nothing wrong. She glowers suspiciously, turning it over and over. She can't believe it is not double-sided, with the Queen on both sides.

Norman's triumph is complete. He has gambled and won. He smirks at Poppy, hoping for some reconciliation. 'I am sure your father approves,' he says. 'He always had the best interests of his family at heart. Many times Ernest and I could not agree but Queen Anne helped us to choose wisely. Isn't that so, dear Edna?'

'Och aye', she replies vaguely, still not certain where she stands.

Poppy is about to put her right about that when Norman suddenly stops smiling. He is listening to noises outside the bungalow, whimpering, scratching and then barking. He frowns. 'That sounds like Winston,' he snaps. 'How did he get out? What's he doing here?' He draws the curtains back and looks out. Sure enough, his dog is yapping at the front door. Poppy keeps a straight face. Aunt Edna is puzzled. 'Did you let him out?' she asks, hurrying to the door. He follows her, irritated and complaining because Winston will have to be chained to his kennel. Suddenly Poppy and I are alone.

'What do we do now?' cries Poppy, wringing her hands.

'Think! He must have switched coins, he wasn't leaving it to chance.'

'How?'

'I don't know!'

'It's all your fault.'

'Mine? Why blame me?'

'You said we should play his game, leave it to Queen Anne.'

'What else could we do?'

'Kill him.'

'Don't be absurd.'

'I hate you!'

'Poppy!' This is serious, doesn't she know I love her? My private world is collapsing, I feel terrible.

Suddenly I realise I am staring at something on the floor, something black and soft. It looks like the velvet purse on the table where Norman has left it. Reeling from Poppy's hammer blows, I can't take it in at first. Are there two velvet purses, two identical velvet purses, one on the floor, the other on the table? What's in this second purse? Crouching under the table, I pick it up and look inside. There is the Queen Anne silver crown, but when I look at the other side the Queen's profile is still there - a double-sided counterfeit! Norman must have kept it up his sleeve and dropped it in the rush to deal with Winston. Aunt Edna is returning. With barely time to put the coin back in its purse, I spring to my feet, concealing the black velvet purse even from Poppy. An avalanche of adrenalin threatens to overwhelm me. Power! It's within my grasp at last!

My Aunt takes no notice of me, she sees Poppy in tearful mood and takes her in her arms.

'Dinna cry, my darling,' she says. 'It really isn't a matter for tears, you know.'

'Oh Mummy, 'sobs Poppy, 'I don't want to lose you.'

'You won't, I promise you that.' Mother and daughter rock together as Norman storms in, irritated by the disruption of his triumph.

'Someone let the dog out!' he snarls. He is looking blue murder at Poppy but suddenly he clutches his wrist, feeling for something that isn't there. He looks up his sleeve. Something is missing but he is not panicking. 'Won't be a minute, Edna. I must have dropped something outside.' Trying to look casual, he is sauntering out when I stop him.

'Is this what you are looking for?' say I, putting the velvet purse next to the other one. He freezes on the spot as I take out the two silver crowns and hand them to Aunt Edna, who looks at them wonderingly, then indignantly and finally sadly. She passes them to Poppy, who holds one crown in each hand, shaking with excitement as she realises their significance. Nobody speaks for a long time. Norman is standing his ground defiantly until Aunt Edna shakes her head and sighs. 'Oh Norman, how could you?' She places her engagement ring on the table.

He starts to defend himself, bristling and pugnacious, but he can see the futility. Head high, trying to maintain dignity, he scoops up the ring and the coins and leaves. His humiliation was so total that we felt quite sorry for him. Maybe his love for my Aunt had driven him to such desperate measures but the deception of his beloved was unforgivable. He walked out of her life and she wasn't sorry, that became very clear.

'Away with you, children,' she confessed with a laugh, 'I wasna marrying that man no matter what that paukie Queen Anne decided. I went along with his game but I always knew I couldna trust him. Ernest had found out he was no Squadron Leader at all, but he never let on for all that. He was fun. I shall miss playing heads or tails with him.'

And she skipped through to the kitchen for the bottle of champagne.

Poppy has been a different girl since we drank the loyal toast. She seems to have more time to talk to me, she thinks I'm much more clever and interesting than she thought. To be honest, since the vanquishing of Norman Fowles she sort of hero-worships me, which is a bit unnerving as I've always been the one for that sort of thing. Nice though.

Dreams in the Night

Janet kept dreaming she was murdering her husband. Not every night, but often enough to cause her to wake with a pounding heart and a sense of déjà vu. She began to dread putting out the light, kissing her husband goodnight and closing her eyes for sleep.

Sometimes she would be clutching a knife, groping through a long dark tunnel dripping with foul liquids, and she could see the pin-prick of light grow until it dazzled her. Suddenly, just as she was going to burst out, a man blocked the exit with his body. She couldn't see his head but knew it was Donald. In the darkness she thrust forward with the knife, till the body fell gushing blood. She woke in terror of what she had done.

Other times she was on a cliff creeping up on a man who stood on the edge. Below the waves silently broke on the rocks. She knew it was Donald though his back was turned. Suddenly she pushed with her arms and he fell, spinning slowly down and she found herself off balance and falling too. But her arms became wing-like and she glided over the sea like a bird.

She was frightened because she knew dreams often were wish-fulfilments and she recognized the hate behind those terrible dreams. Consciousness always brought her to her shocked senses. However unhappy the marriage was, she couldn't murder him!

There were times when she thought she should tell him, casually at the breakfast table, when he was hidden behind the morning paper. 'Oh by the way, Don,' she would say as she spread the marmalade on toast, ' I murdered you again last night.' Or one evening, after he had returned from the building site and sat moodily watching television at bedtime. 'Well,' she might sigh, 'time for me to climb the wooden hill to dream the next exciting episode of Murder in the Sitting-room.'

But he would not be listening, increasingly he turned a deaf ear. Bills and shopping lists seemed their only common interest. He went one way, the managing director of a development company engaged on excavation work for high-rise buildings. She went the other, to the nursery school where she taught the youngest children. 'We both lay foundations!' had once been a joke uniting them.

He was having an affair with a secretary or something. One day, shopping in town, she had casually stopped at the viewing platform of the new development to stare down at the yellow helmets of workers swarming like ants below. She had seen Donald come out of an office with a plan and then a girl had approached him and talked intently. He had touched her arm gently before going back to the office, and instinctively even from that distance she knew.

The dreams were getting more intense. One early morning she woke in terror to find Donald sitting up looking at her oddly. Her dream had been so vivid. She was driving a huge truck, clutching the wheel as it pounded along in the darkness. The headlights stabbed the night and moved about like searchlights. It was empty countryside and a bridge came in sight. A man stood where the bridge arched upwards and she could see the road was broken. He was waving and she knew it was Donald as she drove straight at him because his face caught the glare of the lights. He bounced off and the truck leapt forward into space. She jumped out and fell slowly on to his blood-spattered body. She couldn't tell Donald about it. She lay sleepless till the alarm told her it was time to rise and in the morning he had forgotten the disturbance.

On Friday, after a day at school, she was relaxing in the bath when the phone rang. It was Donald, asking if she had anything on that evening. Wrapped in a bath towel, she listened to him explaining that he would like to take her out. He had been given tickets for the floor-show at the Trocadero. It was a business deal, one of the perks of the excavating job he was working on.

'We haven't been out for ages,' he said, 'and I'm sorry. Maybe this is just what we need to bring us together.'

She was excited, he sounded so cheerful, friendly and she wondered if his little affair with the secretary was over. She agreed to meet him at the station at eight. He would be supervising the final stockpile driving until late but could get a wash-and-brush-up at the hotel. She felt a little self-conscious in her evening clothes on the train but he was there as promised at the ticket barrier, looking spruce in suit and overcoat. He came forward eagerly, his hands grasping hers. They gossiped lightly as he led the way to the car in the station forecourt but she didn't recognize it. Donald drove a BMW, this was a Ford.

'It's a company car,' he apologized. 'Mine's got starter-motor trouble and won't be ready till tomorrow. Never mind, the show starts at nine and it will get us there!'

Parking was a problem though, outside the Trocadero. Donald drove round the block gloomily. 'This is hopeless,' he complained. Just as she saw an empty kerbside, he exclaimed, 'I know! We can use the site parking space – it's just round the corner from here!' And he drove purposefully along a side street, across a small square and up a narrow road with cars and vans parked on either side. There seemed no room there, but Donald pointed where scaffolding and some hoardings blocked the end of the road.

'There's yours truly!' he said, referring to his name emblazoned on the notice board. 'We've got a private car park through the gateway.' Janet could see wooden gates between the scaffolding, and a metal bar across them. 'Be an angel, Janet, open the gates. All you have to do is lift that bar, it's on a swivel. Save time!'

She got out of the car, slightly irritated. She didn't want to break a fingernail or snag a stocking. Stepping gingerly to the gates, she touched the horizontal bar. 'Do I pull this up?' she called, and turned to look into the glare of the headlights.

Suddenly her dreams flashed before her. The alley was tunnel-like, dark and menacing, the lights dazzled her and the roar of the engine suddenly increased. He's going to kill me, she thought, he's driving straight at me! One of the gate swung loosely as she clutched at the bar, the other for some reason jammed, and the car struck it head on, sending both gates flying. But Janet, frantically clutching at the gate, was swung violently out and round. She had a momentary glimpse of a sheer wall and a yawning black space and then the gate in a half-circle hit the back of the scaffold barrier and she was flung against metal poles on the edge of the precipice. For a moment she lay there stunned, while the car engine subsided to a ticking-over and the two gates swung casually back and forwards over space. The headlights glared ahead, then suddenly cut. She heard the car-door open and footsteps approached the brink.

Cautiously she removed her shoes and inched along the scaffolding. There was a small hole in the boarding that formed a wall and she crept through to hide shivering behind a parked van. She could see him peering into the blackness, looking down to spot her body on the concrete below. A muffled curse and he was returning to the car obviously to fetch a torch, for he stood at the gateway, flicking the beam over the ground far below.

She remembered her dream and almost without willing it, found herself creeping up behind him as he concentrated on finding her broken body. With one desperate lunge, she pushed with all her strength and launched him into space. He had no time to resist, he half swung round, lost his torch and then fell, silently and so suddenly that she was shocked by the stillness and loneliness. The hum of the city seemed miles away.

Her dreams! She saw it all now – they were warnings for her, in some miraculous way they were preparing her for this terrible ordeal. It was Donald who was the murderer and he had planned this event so cunningly! Now he lay dead on the foundations of his site, justly killed by his own malice.

She put out her hand to steady herself, groping for the scaffold upright by the gate-side. And missed. Off balance, she leaned forward and suddenly saw before her the bottom of the vast pit with a body spread-eagled. She tried to pull herself back, remembering the dream when she had lost her balance, fallen and floated like a bird.

She fell, instinctively spreading her arms as if they might be wings.

Lord Shiva's Lingam

The sustained cry, a continual monotone, stirs Mrs. Moore from her afternoon siesta. Blankets of sound fold and unfold in her mind but the cry pierces them like a laser and she reverts to being a forty-year widow in India, though she is not back on the plantation but wandering through some exotic Hindu building and then the memory of Sri Meenakshi flickers vividly into focus and she is aware of priests of the temple processing and the wailing cry of supplicants echoing through shadowy corridors, and that one sustained note - OM - droning in her ears, calling to the gods, imploring eternal rest, submitting to whatever was, is and shall be.

The cry stops abruptly. She has just time to wonder why she should dream of Sri Meenashki when the OM call starts again, only this time pitched higher and it makes her cluck to herself irritably. That racket is merely Davy, her great-grandson, howling his head off upstairs. It is nothing like the sacred sound still echoing in her mind. She grunts, unhappy about images from the past. Keep that child quiet! She can hear Clara's voice raised to quell the crying.

Through the French windows she sees the cat, as if impelled by the row inside the house, streak across the lawn to scare a robin picking at a leaf. This must be a special day for the family. Usually when Meg calls with her son Davy, they send him down to talk to his great-grandmother. Not that she cares. What is the point of worrying about the family when she has to prepare for the end? Peace and eternal rest, that is what OM is about and that's what she wants. The crying has stopped. Mrs. Moore settles to brood and doze.

They call her 'Great Gran' upstairs, a kind of distancing name she dislikes; nor did she much care for her daughter Clara, who has become an embittered matron in her middle-age, probably the result of her own daughter Meg going off the rails. Clara rarely visited the garden flat in the afternoon in case she found her mother asleep, slumped in the armchair with head bent at right angles, eyes closed, mouth an ugly slit in the wrinkled parchment of her face and the top of her head revealing bald patches. Afraid to find her mother dead, thinks Mrs. Moore sourly. Then she remembers: today Clara is arranging a birthday party for her.

Clara's husband had maintained his opinion: 'It can't be long now. She's a tough old bird but she won't make ninety,' but he was wrong as usual, of course. His mother-in-law was entering her ninety-first year like a rudderless, derelict craft drifting into port, watched in amazed silence by a few desultory spectators. Even if her mother showed little interest, Clara had decided to celebrate the event.

'Not one word of thanks,' complained Clara to the hired help in the kitchen. 'I told her this morning we would start with champagne and then have smoked salmon sandwiches and petits fours for tea, including her own Deccan hybrid, specially obtained at great expense from the dealers.'

'Lovely,' said Mrs. Higgs.

'You'd think she would appreciate that at least. And then we'll give her a few presents, though goodness knows it's not easy to find what a ninety-year old needs.'

'Is it just the family then?' asked Mrs. Higgs.

'We shall be six, counting mother,' answered Clara. ' My husband is leaving the office early, and my sister and her husband are driving over. And then Meg, our daughter.'

'Ah, you've forgotten someone,' said Mrs. Higgs. 'Davy.'

'Of course – Davy,' exclaimed Clara. 'We'll be six and a half, that's Davy's age too!'

'Bless his little heart,' murmured Mrs. Higgs. 'He does love his great-granny. What's he done with himself now?'

'Silly boy, opening the biscuit tin and making a mess like that! I told him to play in the bedroom with his cars and he seems to have quietened down.'

Adjusting the gladioli in the oriental vase by the front door, Clara entered the sitting-room. Davy was squatting on the rug by the hearth constructing a castle with birthday cards, which he had taken from the window-sill. He was in the middle of a delicate balancing feat and hardly noticed her entry.

'Davy, you naughty boy!' scolded Clara, allowing some of the tensions of the afternoon to spill into a brief shaking of the boy. 'I told you to go to your room and play there, and I find you in here, actually playing with great-gran's birthday cards. They are not yours to play with, and look, you've got dirty marks on one already. That's very naughty, I don't know what your Mummy will say! Go up to your room at once.'

Clara looked at this sullen boy, offspring of her daughter's liaison with a foreign student at college, aware of his beautiful head, the dark lustrous hair and sombre, burning eyes that questioned her. She could not help hardening her heart against him. Because of this child, her daughter had suffered and even now remained single; because of him so many hopes had been abandoned. Then, because he was obeying her order, she relented and told him to sit and watch television, like a good boy. 'I'll just fetch you an orange juice if you promise not to spill it,' she said, and went through to the kitchen.

Davy sulked. Meg, his mother, had left him at granny's because she wanted to do a bit of shopping but nobody was paying any attention to him. He had been told strictly not to go the garden-flat because great-gran was resting and it was her special birthday. So what was he supposed to do? He pressed the ON button and watched a cartoon on the screen but he was restless. Was she asleep? Would she wear a special glittery dress for her birthday? Was he supposed to give her a present?

Downstairs, Mrs. Moore gazes with unseeing eyes at the robin hopping about the lawn. The droning OM echoes down the corridors of her mind, she is back in India, sitting in her favourite rattan chair on the veranda of the bungalow looking at the blue haze of the Nilghery Hills as the sunset touches the crests with gold. The sharp aroma of eucalyptus hangs in the evening air and she hears herself calling to the houseboy: 'Ranjan! Chota peg! Chop chop!' and she watches Ranjan shuffle on to the veranda with a gin and it, smiling and greeting her with 'Hello Esmiss Esmoore, how are you this evening?' And the tea-pickers are bringing their final leaf-filled baskets from the serried tea-bush fields (top two leaves and buds plucked at lightning speed) and the clerks are checking the loads, shouting brusque orders to the women who adjust their saris for the long walk back to town, barely noting the lone figure on the veranda. And she sees the familiar grey dust-cloud as her husband George drives home from surveying the seven thousand acres of the plantation. Their car was an old banger, an Austin, was it? An old sepia film flickers across her mind, a panning shot of the plantation in the thirties, and she is walking towards the little noisy box with its thin tyres and straight black sides, and then she sees herself turn, smile and wave at the camera held – by whom? Not George, he is at the steering wheel, would it be Dennis? A face flashes momentarily, fair wavy hair and a grin with uneven teeth, and fades as she struggles to remember.

What time is it? Afternoon sun outside with bright splashes of colour amid a gentle English greenness. In Tamil Nadu everything will be browns and ochres under a sun glowering like a Hindu deity, fierce and unforgiving. Why is she thinking of Ranjan, her loyal houseboy, devoted to pleasing the memsahib? His wrinkled prematurely old visage is a momentary image – hardly a 'boy' with his wife and children crammed into the converted stable. A sudden memory jolts her senses. 'You're a damned liar, Ranjan! Get out! Out!' shouts her husband. She sees his bulging eyes and flushed cheeks, his mouth in a snarl, striking Ranjan who stands stiffly and silently, looking at her.

Something nags her memory, makes her think of a dark-haired Indian boy, itches like a mosquito bite. She closes her eyes to block out the images but she knows it is all about Dennis, tall and handsome like a hero out of Warwick Deeping or Jeffrey Farnol, riding his pony over from the neighbouring plantation, cheering her up with gallant flattery. She grimaces at the memory of him lying with her under the mosquito-netting and his warm body so close to hers she can't distinguish between them as they merge and Mrs. Moore shudders and begins to remember how she saw a small figure peering into the room from the doorway, white teeth and white eyeballs staring at the naked lovers and then vanishing into the shadows. And the bungalow is strangely quiet, not even the punkah flapping.

Mrs. Moore opens her eyes, needs a drink of water and looks round for the carafe. There is a boy, standing by the door, staring at her.

She knows who it is - Ranjan's son, and she dare not look at him. She hears herself crying, 'No! no!' as George questions the three domestics who shake heads, dumb with fright, and Ranjan falls to his knees. 'No sir!' he cries. 'Memsahib do nothing, I swear no!' And clashing cymbals deafen her as she tries not to listen and stays silent as George dismisses Ranjan and staggers drunkenly from the room, and Ranjan's son is suddenly climbing a donkey-cart piled with meagre belongings to sit beside his mother and Ranjan as they leave the plantation and the boy is looking at her and she can't bear it as he silently implores to - to - to confess?

It was a futile love affair, a fling, she thinks. Sex and love don't last. Dennis joined up to fight in Europe's war and never came back; her marriage to George had to be saved. But she can't bring herself to look round to see if the boy is still at the door. Tears are in her eyes.

There is a soft pressure on her shoulder. The boy is standing close besides her, holding a glass of water and asking, 'Are you all right, great-gran?' Mrs. Moore closes her eyes and returns from the past. She drinks greedily, trying to adjust her thinking. Davy's dark, mobile eyes search her face and, discovering tears, he takes a towel and wipes her cheeks.

'You shouldn't be sad,' he says. 'It's your birthday.'

She remembers. 'Why yes, Davy, I do believe it is!' she cries. 'I'm ninety years old!' And then she clutches his arm compulsively, so fiercely he is frightened. 'But do forgive me, say you forgive me,' she pleads.

'What for?' he asks. He touches her cheek with cool fingertips. He is smiling at her, as if there really is nothing to forgive and she hugs him for comfort.

'Mother, are you awake?' the voice of Clara calling down the stairs. 'Is Davy with you?' Clara bustles into the room, torn between concern for the old lady and anger at the boy's disobedience. 'Meg has just phoned to say she'll be a little late for the party. Typical!' she snaps, wagging a finger at Davy. 'And, young man, I said nothing about the biscuit tin, or the birthday cards, but I shall have to tell her how you disturbed great-gran's sleep on her birthday. It really is naughty of you.'

Mrs. Moore speaks up. ' No, no, he's a good boy!' she cries. 'He's not to blame, let him play in the garden, Clara.'

And Clara, impressed by her mother's concern, opens the french window and ushers him into the enclosed back garden. 'You can pick the daisies on the grass, Davy. I'll show you how to make a daisy chain for great-gran's birthday, that will be a nice present for her! And be a good boy.'

A ring at the front door sent her hurrying from the garden-flat. That would be her sister and brother-in-law and she did want to give them a warm welcome. As for Meg's delayed arrival, there was no telling with that girl.

Mrs. Moore watched Davy pick daisies and tut-tuts as he simply pulls the heads off; he soon loses interest and, wandering down the path towards the shed by the vegetable patch, sits on the step. The robin flies across and settles near him and he lobs daisy heads at it till it goes. He tries the shed door, opens it and enters.

Mrs. Moore sat thinking about the boy. He had touched her face as if to heal her sore memories. There was something very Indian about him, as if the foreign student who had fathered him was Dravidian despite what Meg said. A spasm of self-disgust shook her. Why had she run away from India? Life on the plantation had ended with the Partition and Britain's Exodus though George had wanted to stay on, running the plantation as before, but then he died of typhoid. She couldn't face the new India, self-confidence suddenly deserted her and a year later she had sold the estate to a syndicate of merchants, retiring to obscurity in a Sussex resort with her daughters, both educated and married in England, within calling range. A new life, free from those isolated years on the plantation and yet burdened with half-forgotten, half-suppressed memories. Mrs. Moore sighed with regret: I have measured out my Anglo-Indian years with gins and its.

Movement in the garden distracts her. Davy has found a white powder in a bag. As she watches, he tips some into a shallow tray and carries it to a bucket. Water dribbles. Davy stirs with a stick, so absorbed he gets his clothes in a mess. He seems to have forgotten his great-grandmother and she lapses into a reverie, her thoughts overwhelmed by a succession of vivid images from the temple of Sri Meenakshi. Grotesque carved figures swarm round the towers reaching high above roof-tops; a proliferation of fantastic goblins and satyrs, nymphs and genies, demons and heroes, serpents and monsters, spirits, gods and goddesses dance and writhe as if mocking her ignorance of India's creative imagination. She sees the blackstone bull in a courtyard solemnly scrubbed and stained by attendants, Nandin the bull-god, Lord Shiva's steed as he travels the universe. That was in the guidebook, studied on the train journey to Madurai.

The Club Secretary had leered at her as he explained, 'Sri Meenashki is dedicated to Lord Shiva, the destroyer and preserver, but the place reeks of other gods. The natives have their favourites of course but every true pilgrim wants to kneel before the lingam of Lord Shiva. That's forbidden to non-believers!' And he ogled her suggestively amidst shrieks of laughter from the Club members on the visit when she timidly asked, 'What is the lingam of Lord Shiva?'

'Fools! Fools!' she cries harshly, startling herself into opening her eyes. Davy is patting the tray with a trowel, making what must be mud-pies. Eventually he starts picking up the daisy heads and then breaks off other flowers and takes them to the shed. He fiddles in the tray and she is about to lose patience when the family arrives and advances towards the shed. It is like watching Buster Keaton at the pictures. There is Meg, still in her coat, hurrying to Davy but he scampers out of her arms, pursued by Clara and her sister. The two husbands seem to be guffawing. 'Fools!' mutters Mrs. Moore. Davy is caught, Meg tries to brush the powder off her son's jumper and they all look towards the garden-flat and wave cheerfully at her before marching into the house. Her son-in-law makes gestures - he means to bring the wheelchair in five minutes' time. But she neither waves nor nods, she sinks back into a recollection of a happy Indian

59

outing, projecting on to her mind's screen a vivid memory of an extraordinary Hindu temple exploding with colourful wonders as pilgrims and supplicants flock through the courtyards, prostrating themselves before monstrous deities - a bulky elephant, a grotesque monkey, a menacing blood-stained goddess, a carnival of animals and spirits in a fantastic display of energy.

But why had she suddenly shrunk behind a pillar, gripped by a nausea that made her grope for support? She can remember recoiling from the crowds, glimpsing something in the courtyard that shocks her and makes her run away from her friends, and reject the effort to recall what she has seen. She sips water and then rises, trying to dismiss the vague surmises in her mind. She must get ready for the birthday. As she dabs toilet-water on her dry skin, hanging a string of pearls round her neck, combing her thinning hair, she studies her image, the sad-faced ninety-year old, lined and gaunt, the eyes without lustre, the mouth permanently downcast. Something has oppressed her over the years, deprived her of contentment, sapped her enjoyment of Sri Meenashki. There was a boy, she remembers, but Davy is no longer in the garden nor is he at the door when John arrives with the wheelchair and pushes her along the ramp and into the main house, talking cheerfully and aware that Mrs. Moore is not responding. She won't see ninety-one, he thinks.

Fleeing from that courtyard, she passes through a huge open doorway, watching herself hurry down a long dark hall with mighty pillars, passing prostrate pilgrims and strange effigies, trying to escape from something glimpsed in the courtyard, and gets lost in a warren of corridors that lead to the heart of the temple. Gradually the babble of voices fades and she moves cautiously through curtains and screens and emerges in a silent chamber where sound is muffled and the air heavily perfumed, its stillness and solemnity compelling her to stand motionless and awestruck. In the centre of the chamber a thick brass column, with carved corn-sheaves sprouting round its base, rises arcanely from an ornate metal arch and disappears through the painted ceiling. Four intricately decorated cloth tubes hang limply in the dim spaces surrounding this strange gleaming shaft. Distantly priests are intoning OM and she knows she is trespassing. The wheelchair jolts her and she looks up to face the smiles and greetings of the family in the lounge.

'Happy birthday to you! Happy Birthday to you! Happy birthday, great granny, happy birthday to you!' they chant. 'Ninety years today!' And they start clapping and hugging her as she sits motionless.

She has no right to be here! An outraged priest, naked to the waist, springs from the shades, hissing abuse and pushing her away, and she flees into the maze of corridors, seeking her friends and safety. She can see a group of tourists gathered round a horrible bronze goddess and there are worshippers reverently gazing at the statue and ritualistically flicking red and white pats of grease at it.

'Ah there you are!' calls the Club Secretary, 'Where have you been?' but Mrs. Moore shakes her head, she cannot tell anyone why she has run away and what she had seen in the sacred chamber of the Lord Shiva. The Secretary is ogling her again as he advances to greet her but he is pressing a wine glass into her hand and singing. 'For she's a jolly good fellow, and so say all of us!' And one of her friends buys some pats of the greasy ghee and patronisingly lobs some at the goddess and they all laugh. And she joins in the laughter, intent on wiping out what she has glimpsed in the outer courtyard.

They are all drinking champagne and smiling. Mrs. Moore understands she is in the lounge and watches her daughter unwrap a yellow dressing gown and present it to her, and she smiles and nods her thanks though she already has two hanging behind the door in her flat. Then Clara triumphantly places a large box in front of her but she scarcely realises it contains a video recorder and she cannot comprehend when John tries to show how it works. Her eyes are closing, her pale lips quivering, as if she undergoes some kind of pain. The family look at each other anxiously. Meg gently offers her grandmother a new hot water bottle, already warmly filled, and kisses her. She clutches it gratefully, then lets its slip from her fingers.

Mouth agape, eyes staring into space, she is remembering! Passing through that bazaar-like courtyard swarming with excited, devout worshippers, she had noticed the long line of beggars and mendicants squatting against the wall, extending skinny arms with bowls in hands, and suddenly she had seen, beside a wrinkled, emaciated, half-blind old beggar, a young man whose gaunt features and dark imploring eyes seemed familiar. She knows who he is, this lean, famished youth in rags: Ranjan's son pathetically begging beside that broken diseased old man, and she can't face them. They haven't seen her yet so she hides behind a pillar and runs away through the great door that fronts the inner sanctum of the temple.

'God forgive me,' Mrs. Moore whispers to herself. 'I have lived with such wickedness in my heart. What has it done to me? I am ninety years old and ask that question.'

The family are puzzled by great-gran's mutterings. Perhaps they should start tea, and Clara hurries to the kitchen to warn Mrs. Higgs. Perhaps a suffusion of the special Deccan hybrid will clear mother's mind. Bringing in the salmon sandwiches, she announces, 'Tea is served!'

'Wait a minute!' cries Meg. 'Davy has to give his present first.'

'Can't it wait, Meg dear?' asks Clara. 'The tea's made.'

'Here, old boy,' says John to his brother-in-law,' let's finish the bubbly!' And they clink glasses to great-gran who sits motionless in her wheelchair, still struggling with her past. Then Davy steps forward, holding the shallow tray taken from the garden-shed, advancing to her shyly, his hair clean and brushed, his knees spotless. As he places the tray on her lap, Aunt Susan titters and her husband rolls his eyes

Clara protests. 'Meg, we don't want that messy thing in here, it will drip on the carpet!'

But great-gran is studying the tray, which seems to be covered with flower petals, daisy heads, green stalks and leaves delicately interwoven, stuck down and hiding the cement mixture underneath.

'It's like a mosaic!' cries Mrs. Moore in wonder. She looks at Davy and whispers, 'You made this for me?' Davy nods and Meg crouches by her son and puts her arm round him.

'Do you like it, gran?' she asks.

'I don't deserve it,' she replies, and addresses Davy as if he was not her great-grandson. 'I am truly sorry, you know, but I don't expect you to forgive me.'

Davy solemnly shakes his head. 'Thank you for liking my present, there's nothing to forgive.'

Somewhere inside her a voice, pitched on a monotone, half-droning, half-sighing, is maintaining a sustained note, pronouncing the eternal word, OM, evoking what was, what is and what ever shall be, and what is beyond eternity. It reaches to her senses and touches her inner being. And suddenly there seems a great deal to live for and she hugs Davy and smiles at his mother.

'You have given me the best present in the world!' she says. 'It reminds me of India. Do you know, I went to a wonderful temple called Sri Meenashki in Madurai and, you'll never guess, I actually saw the lingam of Lord Shiva there! That's something to be proud of.' And to the astonishment of the family she started laughing.

Later, son-in-law John commented to Clara, 'Remarkable recovery, I think she's game for another ten years!'

Road Rage

He found driving the Porsche not easy with gout in his left big toe. The clutch pedal was stiff and pressing down sent pains like electric pulses up his leg. He couldn't bear to keep his foot down and the gears jarred and grated. Every time he braked hard, the engine stalled. Yet he had to keep going, reach Brighton by eight and get the stuff unloaded in time for the pay-out. It would be okay as long as he kept out of trouble on this trip, no good ramming someone and getting stopped, not with all that gear in the boot. Just drive easy and avoid the main roads.

He chewed another painkiller, which didn't seem to make much difference. He had woken with the pain throbbing and stabbing as if a trapped nerve was screaming in his left leg. There was no time to see a doctor, and the chemist said it was a hangover. He was all for wiping that smirk off his stupid face with a head-butt. It has nothing to do with the booze last night. The fact is his left toe is a weak spot, ever since he kicked a football about as a kid, but the point being, why should it flare up like a beetroot today, looking like a rancid boil full of pus, when he wasn't doing nothing he didn't do every day? After he had met the van and loaded up, the pain had got worse but he was driving carefully and no speeding. That's how he had got as far as Polegate crossroads and was cutting through to Jevington and Friston, avoiding the big hill out of East Dean. He still had plenty of time, though now the day was over and the light fading fast.

Lowering clouds darkened his outlook. Raindrops speckled the windscreen and head lights dazzled him as cars flashed by. He switched on the wipers and the blur became distinct shapes and beams of light. The on-coming traffic was thinning but there was a regular line of tail lights ahead. The rain suddenly slashed and gusted across the road, bouncing off the windscreen and drumming on the roof. He cursed this unexpected down-pour which came from seaward and swept bleakly across the Downs. In the dusk, his headlights caught sheep huddling under walls or thorn-bushes; a solitary horse blinking in the rain, a car pulled off the road as if broken down. He could see stationary red lights in front and a dark menacing line of vehicles. Some kind of hold-up, perhaps an accident, he would have to slow down.

Gingerly pushing the clutch pedal with his left heel, he tried to engage second gear. Immediately a flash of forked lightning shot up his leg into his spine. His foot recoiled, the clutch slipped back into fourth, his right foot was on the brake pedal but he was still moving too fast. The line of red lights was on the move but not the car in front. He pressed harder on the brake and felt the car sliding forward with locked wheels. It was like watching a slow-motion film sequence, the car in front, a white Citroen 2CV, gradually enlarging, the red tail lights approaching him, his hands gripping the wheel as he hung on, waiting for the bang.

It never came in that split second. His car skidded to a halt an inch from the Citroen's bumper. He had time to open his eyes, take the pressure off the throbbing foot and think he was safe when – his own car exploded with sound and a crunching jolt sent his head jerking backward and his senses reeling. The Citroen leapt forward a couple of yards and just as suddenly stopped. When he thought about it later, that's what saved him from a real mess-up – the driver in front was in neutral with no brakes applied, there was nothing to stop it being shoved along the road. But at that moment he felt like a bag of bones shaken and spilled, ear-drums roaring and head aching, neck cricked, legs paralysed but funnily enough, no pain in the toe. He couldn't think straight but he worked out if he had bounced the Citroen forward, he must have been hit from behind. It took time to realise the consequence of this. He rubbed his aching neck – whiplash. He tried to move and winced as a warning stab pierced his foot. The gout hadn't gone and he leaned over the steering wheel to ease the pain.

A white-haired elderly woman stepped from the Citroen and walked unsteadily towards him in the beam of his headlights, with the rain slashing across her. He waited, knowing he couldn't get out to meet her, not with his problem. The woman bent forward, her white hair halo-ing her pale face, and rapped on the window. Was he all right? she kept mouthing, with the occasional passing car drowning her words.

'Sod off, you silly bitch,' he heard himself muttering, and he was thinking how to guard his left foot, to stop the gout engulfing him, how to keep still so she doesn't know, but now she straightens to speak to someone else. It must be the driver of the vehicle that hit him. When he comes into view, he is a great hulking brute who stands in the headlight shaking a fist, casting a dark shadow over the startled woman. 'You fucking stupid cow!' he bellows. 'Why didn't you get moving? Look what you made me do, you fuc -'

The blaring klaxon of a speeding car drowned the rest of his words. The man's ugly cropped head passed through the headlights, revealing a snarling mouth and glinting eyes. He was threatening to smash the woman's face. She was terrified, motionless, her white coat glowing in the beam of light, like a headless phantom. Traffic streamed by, unconcerned about two blurred figures facing each other in the rain. He knew he ought to get out and help the poor woman but his toe throbbed, as if warning him to lie low.

He wound down the window, feeling the rain stab his cheek and shouted. 'Leave her alone, it's not her fault!' yelling into the wind and roar of a passing car. He regretted interfering at once, for now the thug was coming for him, cursing and blinding. Quickly he closed the side window and locked his door, just in time for the brute began to pound the glass and shake a clenched fist. He could hear the woman crying for help, stepping into the road to wave down an approaching car, and the man swore at her, turned and disappeared from view.

He must have got back into his car because the headlights flickered as the ignition coughed into action. He was revving up, backing and accelerating past the Porsche and the Citroen, nearly colliding with the woman. It was too difficult to make out the car number, the colour, the make, before it drove off into the gloom. With mounting fury, he watched as a car stopped and the woman ran to it, weeping and waving with the rain dripping from her white hair. He realised he was stuck like a bloody pig in the middle. Whatever happened next, he would be seen as villain or coward and, in any case, he didn't want to get involved. He had to get away while he could. Turning off his headlights, he quietly started the engine, gritted his teeth and pressed his left foot on the clutch pedal. The car edged forward and he quickly shot into top gear as the woman and her helper moved towards him. He could see them looking startled and scared as he passed by and accelerated down the road. When he lost sight of the woman in white in the rear mirror he switched on his lights. She had started it, silly cow.

Or he could blame the gout. That's what made him stay in the car. He'd done well to shout at the thug but thank God he'd stayed put. He grimaced at the thought of a hob-nailed boot stamping on his toe. And then, for the first time, he remembered the stuff in the boot. That thug had rammed him and got away with it. What damage had he done to the car? He drew into a lay-by when he was well clear and clambered out of his seat to view the rear of the car. Every step was painful. The on-side rear light was shattered but the bumper seemed okay until he saw it had been pushed into the boot. He couldn't open it. As he hobbled back to his seat, a cold rage settled over his heart, the gout burning with an angry glow. Somehow he was going to get even with that bastard.

Ten minutes later, he passed a car that had stopped by the roadside. The sidelights were on and in the gloom someone was peeing into a hedge. He flashed by, but was struck by a sudden thought - was that the thug? Something about the figure reminded him. He pulled into a lay-by further on and waited for the car to pass by. He caught a glimpse of a cropped head at the wheel and recognized him. Instantly the adrenalin flowed, he was overwhelmed by a compulsion to smash his ugly mug, pulp his body, rip off an ear, kick his ribs in. He followed the car, stalking and planning what to do.

The red-hot pain surged up his leg. He was stupid! The gout was crippling him and he still felt the whiplash injury to his neck. Neither a gun nor a knife was in his car, so what could he do? He glanced at the dashboard clock; still plenty of time before the Brighton meeting. Better stay on the trail, find out where the bastard lives and come back later with a mate or two to fix him and get compensation for repairs. He concentrated on keeping a regular distance behind the car. The rain had ceased and he was now approaching the descent that led to the Cuckmere Haven. To his left he could see the flat estuary where glassy river meanders were dimly lit by an early full moon struggling against dark clouds over the sea. Not a single glimmer out there in the Channel. He felt alone with his quarry as he negotiated the winding road that took him over the narrow bridge way but then he was held up by cars coming the other way. When he got going again, he found the road curled round a bend and there was no sign of his prey when he drove up the hill that led into Seaford. Had the thug accelerated out of sight or turned off the road?

His foot was throbbing, as if craving the amnesia of revenge. He needed to get back on the trail. There was a turning off the main road at the top of the hill probably leading to a few houses or a farmhouse; maybe the car had turned down there. He glimpsed red tail lights disappearing down the lane and cautiously drove between flint-stone walls and silent trees, without headlights, and when he came to a slope in the road he moved into neutral, gliding quietly towards a dark huddle of outhouses or barns. There was a car standing in front of one of the buildings with its headlights starkly illuminating the front of what looked like a garage or shed with one of its doors wide open. No one was about, so he quietly braked where the lane dipped sharply and switched off the engine and sidelights. He could hear loud music clearly coming from the car radio, thumping out a heavy beat as he sat in darkness watching the scene. Suddenly appearing from the pitch black interior of the garage, a thickset man stepped into the headlights and walked through them towards the back of his car. With his cropped head and burly shoulders he was instantly recognisable. He was whistling as he opened the boot of his car and stooped to lift out a heavy box. He was obviously going to carry it into the shed.

As he viewed this from the shadows, an idea began to possess his mind. Why wait? Do it now! The thug was carrying a heavy and bulky box and was concentrating on trying to get his arms round it, testing different grips. He had to put down the box in the roadway, presumably to make sure he was holding it securely. He was facing the shed as he bent forward to pick up the box again. The loud music was muffling all other sounds. With lights off, he gently released the hand-brake and let the car slide forward, gathering speed, and at the very last moment switched on ignition and slammed into fourth gear. Just as the thug lifted the box and took one step towards the shed, the Porsche leapt forward and struck him in the small of the back. He felt the impact as the body buckled and collapsed in front of him. The box was dropped and spilled open, the contents, a computer wrapped in polystyrene moulds, bouncing free. But he hardly noticed as he drove the car forward over the thug, the engine howling as he accelerated away, with the gout pain forgotten in the exultation of success. He remembered he needed lights and switched them on.

The headlights stabbed the darkness and he saw a right-angle bend ahead, a flint-stone wall impassively solid in the glare. He was going too fast. He tried to brake with his right foot, pressed down his left foot on the clutch and felt an agonising pain hit him so abruptly he took his foot of the pedal. The clutch screamed and shuddered as the gear-meshes jarred, and he desperately turned the wheel. He hit the wall at about fifty and the car turned over, trapping him in his seat. He had time to register the total write-off before fury overcame him. He should be in Brighton. He'd miss the deal! Then he lost consciousness.

The Slightly Cross Brigade

*"When I look back on it, I was the one who was angry and
the people I met were more like the Slightly Cross Brigade"*
(Jake Prescott: quoted in The Observer, February 2002)

Jake Prescott told me more about the Angry Brigade, famous for 25
bombings of Tory politicians' homes, government and corporate
offices between August 1970 and 1971. They caused no loss of
human life but the Metropolitan police were tied in knots trying to
locate them. The media had a field day. I don't know who first
called them the Angry Brigade but the members were media icons in
the seventies. Maybe because they were university drop-outs and
cheeky about their political motives, they were different from the
usual subversive terrorists. Comparisons with the German Baader
Meinhoff group or the barricade-building French students in 1969
are unhelpful. The Angry Brigadiers were more like political
saboteurs than terrorists. That's what I suggested to Jake Prescott,
who knew most of the ringleaders. Way back in the seventies he had
been a conditioned drop-out. Having served time for possession of a
firearm, he inevitably gravitated towards life in the squats and
communes of underground London. He got caught up in the heady
revolutionary politics of Trotskyites and that's how he met the
Angry Brigade.

'Saboteurs!' he scoffed. 'You don't know what you're talking
about. They were just part-time revolutionaries, middle-class
libertarian communists dabbling with mass movements without
being seriously committed.' He took a swig of his bitter and added
sarcastically, 'They weren't politically <u>angry,</u> not like me and my
mates were. They were just "slightly cross".'

I said they must have been angry enough to become media icons
and their reputation was founded on successful bombings of
property. No human lives lost!

'So what?' said Jake. 'They were conspiring to cause
explosions likely to endanger life or cause serious injury to property.

71

That was enough to nail them. Actually they were lucky there was no loss of life. They were not half so skilful at controlling explosions as the Crap Brigade. Of course I know all property is theft.'

He lit a fag at this point and noisily inhaled. I realised I was very much out of my depth. 'Have another beer,' I said and we spent some time choosing food from the menu. "The King's Arms" serves a tasty lasagne so we both opted for that. Orders made, I settled back in my corner seat and continued to ply Jake with questions.

'I'm afraid I don't quite understand,' I admitted. 'You seemed to be mentioning some other subversive left-wing group. What did you call them – the Crap Brigade?'

Jake took his time downing the beer. He knew I was ignorant about the seventies, being more like a cub reporter looking for a scoop than a proper journalist. He gazed at me shrewdly, probably weighing up how much his story was worth. He seemed to decide to treat me gently.

He said, 'Yeah, the Crap Brigade. A maverick group working along the South coast, a bit regional so the police were able to hush up the trial. Just four of 'em, all university drop-outs but not half as newsworthy as the Stoke Newington lot, that's where the Bomb Squad arrested the Angry Brigade. The Crap Brigade got their come-uppance in Eastbourne. Different situation, same procedure - after arresting them, the police planted a small arsenal of weapons and explosives in their hide-out. It was a try-out for the Guildford Four and the Birmingham Six arrests. Dodgy evidence but they got away with it.'

'Not in the long run,' I said, recalling how prison sentences had been quashed many years later. 'What were they doing in Eastbourne? Funny place for a revolutionary gang to operate, what with its reputation for respectability and aristocratic connections – the Dukes of Devonshire having laid out the town and all that.

'Ah,' said Jake. 'It was them Dukes got the Crap Brigade going. I was bumming around in Eastbourne at the time.'

'Is that what they called themselves?' I asked incredulously.

'Hang on a minute and I'll tell you all about it,' Jake replied.

The lasagne had arrived and we decided to eat first. Parmesan cheese sprinkled, we gulped our beer and set to. "The King's Arms" was filling up but the two of us were tucked away from the main swarm, quietly forking the delicious pasta dish. Jake ate slowly; I had finished long before him, and sat eagerly awaiting his account of the happenings in Eastbourne. At last he was ready and I recorded his words.

'There were four ex-students, two boys and their girl-friends, squatting in a disused, broken-down house on the edge of the Flatulent estate. That part of town had a reputation for yobboes and street-kid gangs but no one knew this lot was there. It was here they planned to blow up the Duke of Devonshire, and they must have assembled the gear for the bomb there. Obviously they had the know-how to detonate explosives. When the eighth Duke toppled, it was a complete surprise. He stands monumentally on Western Lawns facing the Grand Hotel and that night, just as Lord Snowcap was shuffling out of the Grand in his slippers for his normal prowl along the sea-front, there was a explosive burp, a flash of light and a puff of smoke. Lord Snowcap was knocked off his feet, more or less incapacitated until the night porter rushed out in response to the sudden disturbance, but the Duke of Devonshire was actually knocked off his pedestal. There for all to see (if they could in the dark) was the stone plinth looking totally unmoved and at its side stretched decorously over ten horizontal feet was the intact body of the Duke, lying as if tired out after ninety years standing on parade.

'Lord Snowcap suspected footpads but he was unharmed. A courting couple got caught flagrante delicto in a sea-front shelter as the bomb went off. They tried to blame an ex-boy-friend but he had an alibi, being at home with his mother. The cops brought in three down-and-outs who fell off benches by the Wish Tower but no arrests were made. Forensic tests on the four-letter word CRAP sprayed on the stonework with red paint revealed nothing, 'cos it was common to a lot of teenage vandalism. The Chief Constable was unable to pin the blame on anyone in particular. The usual suspects at the time were ruled out, there being no animal or Irish connections. No one claimed responsibility but people couldn't help admiring the expert way semtex had been tucked in a crevice under the Duke's left shoe, a nicely calculated location for maximum impact on the base of the figure. No one was injured. The Chief Constable decided the attack was the work of a lone nutter and the local paper stopped reporting speculations.

'There was of course uproar in Council meetings but all sides agreed that the Duke should be reinstated. After all, the Devonshire family was not only a prominent landowner but also principal benefactor of the town. In no time at all, the Duke was hauled back into place, an *eminence gris* in academic garb solemnly eyeing the eminent Grand Hotel which spread its wings before him.'

Somewhat surprised by this flighty metaphor, I suspected Jake Prescott was fabricating flowery detail and not telling me the plain, unvarnished truth. He was taken aback by my implied criticism and apologised for getting carried away in his enthusiasm for a tale well told. He defended his account of the Grand Hotel (after all, he said, the building does have two wings) but promised to keep to the point, so I re-started the recorder.

'A couple of months later, this mysterious dissident group struck again. The bronze statue of the eighth Duke's father further along the seafront was blown, if not to smithereens, at least up. This wasn't so successful, though, because of contrasting poses of the two bigwigs. Whereas the eighth Duke was vertically upstanding, the seventh Duke had been sculpted sitting in a wide chair with curved back, looking a bit like Rodin's Penseur only a bit more depressed and he was wearing a gown draped over all. Obviously this broad base made toppling impossible but the seventh Duke was made to look like a Paolozzi objet trouvé.'

'A what?' I queried. 'I don't understand the relevance. Stop messing me about. I want the facts. Tell me the truth!'

He gave me a pitying look.

'Young man,' he sighed. 'I may have been a dropout when I was your age, but at least I have attended Art Appreciation classes in my middle age. All right, forget I said that. The point is, again there was no loss of life, unless you count a gull squatting on the Duke's head, but there was trouble with hoteliers and their guests. A lot of windows were shattered and the noise disturbed their sleep. People started nattering about the competence of the local constabulary. How to protect the town's reputation for peace and quiet and what was being done to arrest any yobbos hanging about?

'The similarity between these attacks upon two generations of a very distinguished family led the Police to make discreet enquiries in Derbyshire. Was everything all right at Chatsworth? Any suspicious characters prowling round the gardens? But no one seemed worried by the goings-on in East Sussex. Still, when the Chief Constable stood up to speak to a packed audience at the Town Hall, with representatives from neighbouring police forces present, there was intense interest.'

I intervened at this point. '"They didn't let you in, did they, Jake?'

'No,' he replied, 'but I know someone who was there. He represented the Street Cleaners Union, there was a lot of debris to clear up. He told me what the Chief Constable said.

'"Gentlemen!" he declared, ignoring several ladies, and one or two ennobled personages, "lightning may strike twice in the same place but surely not thrice. Eastbourne has no more Dukes on parade, but the serial bomber, if this is what he is, may find other targets elsewhere. This town is not unique in honouring the peerage – indeed our aristocracy, even Royalty!"'

'A ripple of unease spread round the room. Police Chiefs from Brighton and Bognor Regis, with their monarchic connections, eyed each other with alarm. How safe were their royal statues? Surely they would not need to mount guard over them? The Press pestered him for more information but the Chief Constable brushed them aside.

'I have my own agenda,' he said. 'Time will tell.'

'And indeed it did. Two weeks later, at North Gate, Brighton, George IV suddenly developed a list to port as a result of a violent explosion. No one was hurt as this incident occurred at dead of night. There was a four-letter word, CRAP, scrawled on the damaged plinth but no one thought this more than coincidence. The Chief Constable issued a bulletin in which he announced that the nutter-bomber would soon be arrested. He was bluffing of course.

'But then two things happened. The first was Mandy Sykes finding a bit of torn paper lodged in the breeches of His Majesty.'

At this moment in the proceedings, Jake Prescott stopped to take another drink. When he was ready, he fixed his gaze upon me. 'I don't suppose you've heard of WPC Mandy Sykes?' he said. 'Mandy who?' I replied.

'Lovely girl,' he murmured and sighed nostalgically. 'She was responsible for getting me out of remand and into that squat. In those days WPC Mandy Sykes, assigned to the CID, was doing good work along the south coast snuffing out drug dealers. She was in Brighton at the time George the Fourth got blown up and went along to survey the scene of the crime. She spotted the scrap of paper inside the ripped breeches and, climbing up the shattered body, pulled it out. It was the top of a letter that was torn across so you couldn't read more than a few words. And d'you know what it said? I'll show you a photo-copy.'

Jake felt in his pocket and unfolded some notepaper. I could read what it said as he spoke the words.

The Campaign for Removing Aristocrats Peaceably
CRAP Headquarters: 23 …

Obviously the address was incomplete.

'Well, you can guess what happened after that. The Chief Constable realised there must be more than one nutter – it must be a gang of nutters. But he didn't tell the Press. Instead he briefed a CID squad to explore every avenue, street, road, crescent, close and lane that had a house number 23, not just in Brighton and Eastbourne but all towns and villages in Sussex. He got plain-clothes detectives to call at local printer firms to check on type faces and orders. They actually uncovered quite a lot of suspicious goings-on but nothing relevant to CRAP. So the Chief Constable held a secret meeting for all personnel concerned in the research, and it was Mandy Sykes who stood up to point out that maybe the house number was not 23 but 230 to 239. The search started up again.'

I interrupted Jake here. 'I thought you said there were two things that changed the way the Chief Constable organised operations. You've only mentioned one.'

'All in good time,' said Jake. 'I was coming to that. I need a leak, excuse me.' Whether he really wanted to go or was just keeping me waiting I don't know, but while he visited the Gents I thought about the strange way that piece of paper tantalised the police – had it been deliberately torn across to conceal the address? I asked Jake about that when he returned.

'Sheer chance if you ask me,' he replied, 'though the Crap Brigade were real teasers.'

Settling back in his seat, he continued his story. 'Anyway, the Chief Constable had an idea that dramatically changed events. He was impressed with WPC Mandy Sykes, she was obviously a bright spark. Why not appoint her as an undercover agent with special instructions to infiltrate the CRAP organisation incognito, send her underground and see what more she can reveal?

'He interviewed her personally. Yes, a good choice, not too tall, not too short, not too old, not too young but just right, with medium brown hair and a very nice smile. He briefed her for the operation. She was to go native, take lodgings in one of the down-town areas, frequent the bars and pubs, go to discos and clubs, attend pop and rock concerts, smoke a bit of pot and stay up half the night probing the dark corners of the underworld and report back after a couple of weeks. Actually this meant little change to Mandy's life-style so she took the job, pleased really to get official approval and most of her expenses paid.'

I had to intervene at this moment. I couldn't believe the Chief Constable would employ such an inexperienced weirdo on an operation like this. Jake fixed me with a scowl.

'Mandy is a lovely lady, don't you call her that,' he growled, squaring his shoulders ominously. 'Maybe she was street-wise but that was what was wanted, see.' I remained silent; perhaps I was being over-hasty in judging Mandy Sykes and Jake continued.

'It didn't take long for her to sink to the lower depths of Brighton but the trail went dead. No one had a clue about the Crap Brigade, not even the rap singers. Mandy moved on, trawling through the south coast towns without catching so much as a crab. And then, the phone rang and she was told to get to Bexhill-on-Sea where Queen Victoria had been assaulted and left severely damaged. The usual situation – night time, no casualties, no warning and the word CRAP sprayed on the pedestal, but this time there was a notice pasted to the plinth. You want to know what it said? It really got them thinking.'

Jake pulled papers out of his pocket and showed me the announcement that said:

CRAP!
Manifesto of the
Campaign to Remove Aristocrats Peaceably

We, the undersigned, hereby proclaim our loyalty to the future of the Citizens of Great Britain. We are peace-lovers and intend no violence against anyone but we believe the following facts:

• Royalty must be abolished and with it the whole apparatus of Hereditary Peers. Noble peers are an anachronism in a modern democracy. Hereditary Peers should lose their special and exorbitant privileges.

• The 600 titled so-called aristocrats and the five degrees of Noble Peers: Dukes, Marquises, Earls, Viscounts, Barons along with non-noble inherited Baronets, must be expunged. These constitute so-called 'High Society' as if 98.5 % of the people do not count!

• 6,000 landowners (mostly aristocrats) own two-thirds of total British land. 70% of land in Britain is owned by less than 1% of the population. Land must be re-distributed so that people have a stake in their own country.

• People are under the tyranny of the landlord. Most home-owners pay heavy taxes and rates, whereas wealthy landowners pay no rates and get grants and subsidies for owning land.

• The poor must no longer subsidise the super rich.

Signed: Dominic d'Underhead, Roger de Montford,
Jessie Matthews, Sandy Soil.
(*Partners in the Campaign to Remove Aristocrats Peaceably*)

Long Live the Republic! Down with Hereditary Peers

'Well, the Chief Constable couldn't keep all that under his helmet. The Crap Brigade was front-page news, but you could tell from the names they weren't to be identified. I called them 'the Fearsome Foursome' but I hadn't a clue. All sorts of people, clairvoyants, astrologers and psychoanalysts among them, tried to reveal their identities. The word 'crap' became an even more popular graffiti message and inevitably there were copy-cat attacks on the statues of certain hereditary peers throughout the country though the Home Office tried to pooh-pooh any suggestion that the campaign was coordinated. Extra watch was kept on all aristocratic-looking statues in parks and public places. Questions were asked in Parliament and the Prime Minister tried to assure nervous MPs that the whole thing would blow over if denied the oxygen of publicity. However, the House of Lords sat for an unprecedented five hours debating the threat to the peerage; and the proprietors of 'Burke's Peerage' offered a reward of a parcel of land, or a coat of arms, to anyone providing evidence that led to a conviction. There were calls for the resignation of the Chief Constable, which really annoyed him because the Crap Brigade was hardly his fault. In fact, if anybody was to blame it was his undercover agent, Mandy Sykes, who clearly wasn't up to the job. She kept asking for expenses and discovered nothing in return. That was his view and he called in Detective Sergeant Blake, i/c CID investigations of South Coast subversive activities, to discuss what they should do about her. They decided to sack her and DS Blake was dispatched to inform her that she should report back to HQ at once.

'It was at this point Mandy got her first break-through. She told me that one Sunday evening while she was on duty in Eastbourne, gloomily sipping a gin and bitters in 'The Crown' in Old Town, she became aware there were four student-types on stools at the bar and they seemed pretty sloshed. There was a ginger-haired bloke with specs, a bald guy with a bit of a belly, and two girls, one blonde, one brunette. They were enjoying themselves, trying to recite a list of Kings and Queens, cheering every time they named a monarch, chanting 'Willy, Willy, Harry, Stee/ Harry, Dick, John, Harry Three/one two three Neds, Richard Two …' but struggling a bit through the middle order and stumbling over Edward VIII with a special cheer for Wallis Simpson before racing to the end. 'Long live Elizabeth the Second!' they cried. The four student-types were falling about with laughter, which seemed to irritate Joe the publican because he told them to shurrup or get out.

'Scum!' he called them, 'I'm fed up of you layabouts using my pub to say rude things about the Royal Family. Where's your respect for your betters eh?' 'Aha!' chortled the gingerhead, 'A publican but not a republican!'

'The students seemed to find this very funny but Joe had had enough. 'Geddoutov it!' he shouted and then the bald one called, 'Last Orders please! Closing time at The Crown!' and the four of them solemnly clinked glasses. Mandy thought they were just stupid, because it was far from closing time. Irritated, she trudged back to her lonely lodgings in Victoria Drive.

'"Bomb in Pub!" screamed the headlines next morning. It was on the radio news. Mandy listened with amazement. "The Crown Public House in Old Town, Eastbourne, was wrecked last night after fire broke out in the saloon bar. Foul play is suspected. The publican and his wife had a narrow escape." Mandy waited no longer. Woman's intuition told her she could crack this, she knew who was in the Crap Brigade and she had to expose them because if aristocratic pubs were going to be targeted, where would the Campaign to Remove Aristocrats Peaceably end?

'Feeling thirsty, she hurried to the scene of the crime but the police had cordoned off "The Crown". She could see various white-clad figures propping up the bar looking for clues but it was best not to join them because she was under cover. It was a pretty desolate scene, with smoke still rising from the debris. Detective Sergeant Blake was holding an impromptu interview with the Press in the ruined parlour but when he saw her he waved as if he wanted to speak to her. Reluctantly she waved back.

'Got news for you, Mandy!' he shouted. She couldn't ignore him though she didn't want to get mixed up in any police enquiry at "The Crown". He handed over a letter from the Chief Constable. She was being taken off the Crap case and must report back to headquarters immediately. Bang goes her life-style, and her chances of solving the mystery. Now Mandy was no fool. She was on the verge of total success. Her task was quite clear: she had to track down the four dangerous criminals before more damage was done. She would unmask them by herself, remaining incognito in order to continue her investigation, and had already decided her next step, which was to seek out the local pubs named after royalty, peers and aristocrats. Yellow Pages obliged her with a working list and she began her gory task. This, she thought grimly, would be the most important pub-crawl of her life, starting with the "Prince Albert" within a stone's throw of the damaged "Crown". She dropped the Chief Constable's summons in a waste bin and got down to work.

'There was one pub name which intrigued her – "The British Queen" in Lower Willingdon, a mock-Tudor edifice. Which queen was this celebrating? How would the Crap Brigade regard this title? Recalling how the fearsome foursome had cheered (or jeered) Elizabeth the Second in "The Crown" it seemed to Mandy that they might launch their next attack upon a contemporary target, as Elizabeth Windsor was still very much the "British Queen". She made plans to visit this pub later in the evening; meanwhile there was a local shop that sold t-shirts and she wanted to dress for the part. She chose a red number with 'Power to the People' printed across the front and took a taxi to Lower Willingdon. She felt like bait dangled to catch a pike but how else could she get a line on the gang? And then, as she was walking in the gloom across the "British Queen" car park, her heart pounded with excitement for there, right before her, was a man, a young man with ginger hair, pacing up and down, as if waiting for friends to arrive. Or was he measuring the front of the pub to calculate firepower later on? Mandy dodged behind a Rover and watched the man; he was the student type all right but it was too early to approach him. And then, puttering into the car park came an old Citreon 2CV and inside she could see three people. Yes! The bald guy, the blonde and the brunette stepped out and greeted the ginger man. Then, huddled together, they entered "The British Queen" and made a beeline for a quiet corner which was perfect for planning a plot and also for making a quick getaway. Mandy knew her hunch had paid off!

'She waited a while by the entrance and then casually strolled in and moved over to the bar where she sat on a stool. Not many customers were about and the barman was polishing glasses absent-mindedly, but it wasn't long before the bald guy came to the bar for drinks. Mandy gave him a good profile view of herself and then flashed a kind of shy little smile at him. It was obvious he was interested in her as he read the message.

'Power to the People eh! Attagirl!' he quipped, eyes gleaming. The barman was taking his time so Mandy gave a little giggle and archly asked the bald guy if he was one of the People. It wasn't long before they were swapping quotes from Marx and Engels, and Chairman Mao and Fidel Castro. Daring to provoke him, Mandy said a few sarcastic things about the Royal Family and the House of Lords. And then, seeing how he was reacting, she leaned provocatively towards Baldy and whispered she was actually an admirer of the Crap Brigade and would love to meet any of them. Mandy could tell he was dying to tell her, "Well, as a matter of fact I am one!" When he took the drinks back to his friends, she saw out of the corner of her eye he was excitedly telling them all about the girl with 'Power to the People' across her front. She ordered a fruit juice and waited patiently. There was a tap on her shoulder and who should it be but Detective Sergeant Blake, CID, grinning at her.

'Go away!' she hissed. 'I'm busy!'

'So this is how you spend your evenings, is it!' he joked, but then added, 'What about that message from the Chief? You left it in a waste bin at "The Crown".' And he held out the letter for her to take.

'Shove off!' she raged. 'You're spoiling things.' And refused to take it or speak to him. DS Blake was hurt but decided to leave her alone, he knew Mandy could be a spitfire. In any case, the ginger student was now approaching and asking if she would like to join his friends in the corner. Without so much as a glance at DS Blake, Mandy was on her way with a big smile, shaking hands and being introduced to Gerard (ginger), Basil (bald), Dawn (blonde) and Deirdre (brunette). It was almost as if the four Brigadiers wanted to welcome a fifth member into their midst, as if they wanted to show off to someone they could trust.

'We are peace-loving republicans who want to get rid of parasitic aristocrats without bloodshed!' she was told.

'We believe there should be severe restrictions on how much wealth should be handed down from generation to generation.'

'Oh I quite agree,' said Mandy.

'That's why we have started the Campaign to Remove Aristocrats Peaceably.'

'Can I join too?' asked Mandy. 'I agree with everything you say.'

'The four of them exchanged glances. They asked her to go for a stroll while they conferred so she went to the loo, passing DS Blake, who seemed to be hiding behind a palm tree, without a word. He could spoil everything with his big boots. On her return he had disappeared but the Crap Brigade were all smiles, having agreed to welcome her to meetings.

'But you must swear an oath of allegiance to the cause,' said baldy Basil. 'The sooner the better.'

'Why not now?' said Dawn. 'Can you spare an hour?' asked Dierdre. 'We need to go to our headquarters for this ceremony,' said ginger Gerard.

Trembling, Mandy nodded and prepared to leave "The British Queen". She was taking a big risk and all on her own. Who would know where she was going? Would she get out of this alive? They travelled in two cars, Mandy the passenger in Gerard's MG saloon while the others chugged along in the 2CV. Eventually they drove down a dismal, deserted street with no lamplights and stopped outside a derelict house that was boarded up and the garden like a tip. The night sky looked just as miserable and poverty-stricken as the surroundings. They entered through a broken back-door and sat on boxes in a circle. The room smelled damp and pungent but a few candles and night-lights created a cheerful and spooky atmosphere. Dawn let down a lop-sided blind that screened the window adequately. Someone produced a bottle of whisky and handed it round. At least that warmed her up a bit.

'We are in 235 Coronation Street on the Flatulent Estate,' said Gerard. 'The Headquarters of the Campaign to Remove Aristocrats Peaceably. Welcome!'

'Before the Oath,' explained Basil, 'you must answer the four questions that will be put to you by saying, "I do". Do you understand?'

'I do,' said Mandy, not really sure she did. .

'Right,' said Dawn. 'I shall read to you the first clause:

Do you agree that Great Britain is a Democratic country that should elect its leaders according to the free vote of its citizens? Therefore the principle of hereditary status and wealth afforded to a few privileged people is irrational and immoral?'

'I do agree,' Mandy said confidently.

'My turn now,' said Deirdre. 'This is the second clause:

Do you agree that Great Britain should abolish the Monarchy and Hereditary Nobility and should become a Republic which elects its leaders by democratic vote?'

'I certainly do,' cried Mandy happily. 'Vive la Republique!' Which was greeted with murmurs of approval from the others.

'Quiet please!' called Basil. 'You must listen to this one carefully.

Do you agree that Land reform is essential because the present system of land ownership favours peers and aristocrats who control land rentals and usage to their own advantage and who cause Great Britain to be uncompetitive and economically hampered as well as unjust to most people and that the Land Registry should complete its work?'

'Yes, I think so,' agreed Mandy a little more cautiously, 'though I don't know about that last bit.'

'Up to 50% of the land in England has still not been registered and evaluated,' said Basil sharply. 'Think what that means to future house-building costs. The failure to get on with Land Registration is an absolute disgrace.'

'Mandy could only nod her head in agreement while Gerard prepared his piece.

'And finally,' he said, 'this clause:

> *Do you agree that as a nation we are being ripped off by the privileged members of our community and that, in addition to weeding out aristocrats from the House of Lords, we should be doing all we can to further the cause of the Campaign to Remove Aristocrats Peaceably.'*

'Definitely, yes I do,' Mandy replied. There was a short round of applause as she signed a document to mark the occasion.

'Solemnly they returned the papers to an orange box and joined hands to sing the Internationale sotto voce. Then they embraced each other in silence, forming a circle in the middle of the room. Mandy felt quite emotional about it, they seemed such nice people dedicated to their chosen cause and then she began to worry about her role as traitor, deceiver, hypocrite. How could she betray them so ruthlessly? But then, once the ceremony was over, they began to discuss the next bombing operation and she knew she had to play this part, they had to be brought to justice before matters got worse. Gerard was urging them to move on, before the police sussed out their hideout. What about Hastings? That's where it all started, he argued. William the Conqueror and Domesday! A Norman's home is his castle! The henchman's reward – a title and land to go with it! There must be a statue or a pub to work on in Hastings. Four heads nodded in response; it was time to seek pastures new.

'Suddenly, as if by design, light blazed outside the house and huge shadows were cast on the walls of the room. An alien voice, nasally pinched through a loudhailer, rang out.

'This is the Police! Lay down your arms and walk out with your hands in the air. You are under arrest. We have you surrounded!'

'Hurriedly diving to the floor, they crawled round blowing out candles and night-lights but the glare from outside was too strong. The hard light on their faces, with pop eyes and gaping mouths, made them look like white clowns. Cautiously Basil looked through one of the slats of the blind and immediately ducked down again.

'It's the police!' he cried stupidly. 'All over the place!'

'Dawn and Deirdre clasped each other, terrified. Gerard crouched in the shadows, a thin smile playing over his lips as he stoically contemplated arrest.

'The disembodied voice boomed again. "Come out of the backdoor, one by one. Keep your hands above your head. Now!"

'Mandy was on the horns of a dilemma. Should she at once reveal herself as an undercover agent and risk assault by the gang of four? Or should she pretend to surrender to the police? Perhaps she could help to prevent any desperate and foolhardy attempt to escape arrest by leading the way through the backdoor. Quickly she moved along the corridor and, flinging the door open, stepped out into the stabbing glare of a searchlight. Before she had time to do more than shield her eyes, she was hurled to the ground by two hulking constables and lost consciousness with a severe blow to the head.

'When she came to her senses she was in hospital and had difficulty remembering all that had happened. Of course the members of the Crap Brigade had surrendered peaceably. The mystery of the south coast bombing attacks was solved and the perpetrators brought to justice. The Chief Constable was knighted and was pleased to receive plaudits for his planning of the capture though he was generous enough to give some credit to DS Blake who had stalked the villains after they left "The British Queen". He had been ordered by the Chief Constable to ensure that PWC Mandy Sykes actually reported to headquarters now she was being taken off the case, being useless as an undercover agent. Being a sensitive officer, DS Blake had not wished to upset Mandy when she was obviously in a bad mood at the pub and had decided to bide his time when the ginger man invited her to join his friends. Lurking in a corner, he had overheard the conversation about monarchy and the aristocracy and, when she voluntarily left "The British Queen" in their company, was uncertain whether she had been won over by their treasonable talk or was pretending. After all, Mandy had refused point blank to speak to him. So, stealing a bicycle left in the car park, he had pedalled after them and kept them under surveillance as far as the empty house near the Flatulent estate. Once the Crap Brigade were inside their headquarters, he had called for reinforcements.'

There was silence as Jake Prestcott finished his beer and rubbed his hands.

'So that was that,' he said. 'And d'you know where Mandy Sykes was when she took the lid off this can of worms? In custody! I was visiting a pal, and there she was behind bars wanting to tell me.'

'I don't believe it! Mandy Sykes deserved a medal for her part in the Crap Brigade arrests.'

'The trouble was,' said Jake, 'nobody knew who was telling the truth. All the members of the Crap Brigade swore that Mandy was one of them. They couldn't believe she was putting on an act in "The British Queen" and the empty house. She took an Oath of Allegiance, didn't she? Maybe they wanted to get their own back on her too. Mandy could have been up for trial. Nobody spoke out at first. Even DS Blake couldn't be certain whose side she was on.'

'But the Chief Constable,' I protested, 'he knew she was an undercover agent!'

'Yeah, funny that,' said Jake. 'he spoke up eventually, after his knighthood, and she left the court without a stain on her character. It got quite romantic. DS Blake fell on his knees apologising to her, he felt that guilty, and while he was there he proposed to her. Mandy had had a basinful of police work so she accepted. Got two kids now, one of each.'

'Those four ex-students,' I said, 'what were they really like?'

Jake smiled. 'Not my cup of tea, you might say. Someone ought to research 'em, find out what was missing from their upbringing. Nice kids, but – well, you know, just slightly cross.'

'What happened to them?'

'Guilty as charged. Six years for the boys, three for the girls. But they got off lightly, the cops released them, after a year. Dunno why, next thing was they were out, re-instated, separated, disappeared. I reckon one of them had friends in high places. Aristocratic perhaps.'

'Why is it we don't know about all this?' I asked.

'Who's 'we'?' replied Jake ruefully. 'Some people know and want it kept quiet. Sort of conspiracy of silence. Hush up the Campaign to Remove Aristocrats Peaceably, just in case their Manifesto might catch on. I blame the hereditary peers. Maybe it's not all crap.'

We drank to the silent majority.

'Now then,' I said, 'tell me about the Angry Brigade ....'

Caviare to the General

I had been hitchhiking most of the morning, quite successfully. Each time I stood by the roadside, rucksack on my back, signalling with the auto-stoppeur's arm, a vehicle stopped either out of pity or curiosity. First, a bright red Citroen 2CV driven at breakneck speed by an eccentric old lady, anxious to reach the market in the next town, with a crate of hens clucking on the back seat. Then, a dirty lumbering camion with a cargo of wooden props that seemed so likely to shift as we negotiated bends in the road that the swarthy driver, cursing continually, refused to open up the throttle beyond 40 kph. And thirdly, making up for slow progress along the route nationale, a Peugeot saloon took me as far as ... all the way to ... a good hundred kilometres south, but well off the main road … to a sleepy little village I had not intended to visit.

When this car drew up alongside me, the driver leaned across the empty passenger seat, wound down the window and hurled a question at me. I had no clue what he said, he spoke so rapidly, but I knew from the upward inflection it was a question, and there was an urgency in his voice. It so happened that I was holding a road map as I bent forward to say 'Qu'est-ce-que - ?' and he indicated impatiently that he wanted to look at it. His finger followed a line and he suddenly exclaimed 'Mon Dieu! Si loin!' as he stabbed the map. He looked at me closely and for the first time it dawned on him I was not French. 'Anglais? Vous voulez l'autostop?' he snapped. 'Oui!' I replied in impeccable French. 'Ascendez!', and gratefully I climbed into the passenger seat.

I became the navigator after that. He was trying to reach a small village with the name St Jean de Lac, obscurely located up a minor road off the route nationale fifty kilometres from Avignon. He was in one hell of a rush and he needed me to check the junctions and the turning-off points. Obviously he had an important appointment to keep in this place but he said nothing about it, just kept his eyes on the road as we zoomed along and muttered to himself. We passed through small towns and villages, and I checked their names on the map. Every now and then I would glance at him, trying to work out what his job was and why he was so anxious to reach St Jean de Lac. He was well built, slightly portly, dressed in a dark suit, balding and clearly a professional man, though I couldn't decide which. There was an odd contrast between his loose fleshy lips, which he kept licking with his tongue, and the sharp eyes that rarely blinked, as if he was concentrating his thoughts but he couldn't control his feelings. He wasn't interested in me, only so far as I could help, and frankly I didn't think much of him. He seemed to be excluding all contact with the world except this one, single journey which he had to complete before it was too late.

Having veered off the main road, we drove along pleasantly shady lanes with pollarded limes lining the route. The sun glinted between the trunks, dazzling us as if a bright light was switched on and off. This was a tranquil landscape, the fields stretching far away with no sign of human activity until we passed a horse and cart, with a youth standing upright holding reins in one hand and a whip in the other. Soon we were approaching a cluster of buildings and reading the wayside signpost that proclaimed 'St Jean de Lac'. My companion uttered a hearty exclamation and for the first time smiled at me. 'Voici St Jean de Lac!' he said, rather unnecessarily.

The road narrowed and curled round dilapidated cottages that must have pre-dated the Revolution, until unexpectedly there was an open space, cobbled and square-shaped. This was clearly the village centre. Surprisingly six or seven cars lined up to one side and as we parked beside them I noticed they were smart, up-market models, more used to gracing the boulevards of Paris than an obscure rustic village square. Two buildings dominated the Place: to one side the village Church, with obligatory crucifix and a notice board with papers flapping in the breeze. Opposite was an extraordinary structure that appeared to be covered with bougainvillaea in full bloom, the scarlet flowers cascading in profusion down the foliage. Perhaps this had once been a farmhouse, with strong timbers, local brick walls, casement windows, and a front door opening straight on to a yard. Now you approached it through an arcade, and it was quite definitely a Restaurant. There was a veranda with tables and chairs arranged at intervals, and a glazed Menu board stood proudly beside the entrance.

It was at this Restaurant that my companion was now gazing, his arms outstretched as he chuckled and roared, for there was a man advancing to greet him, whooping his pleasure at our arrival. I was totally forgotten. I watched as the two men, arm in arm and bursting with laughter, entered the Restaurant and disappeared from view. I could hear some sounds of applause from a room in the recesses of the building and then silence. I slung my rucksack on my back, uncertain what my next move should be. To be dumped so abruptly, without so much as a word of thanks, was irritating. And I had been taken miles off course and up a backwater. I needed to get back on the route nationale.

There was a shout. My erstwhile companion was beckoning, waving me over to the veranda where he stood. He shook my hand, thanked me and demanded that I should sit and have a drink. I expected him to stay with me but, as soon as I accepted his invitation and asked for a bière, he was saying au revoir, shaking my hand again, and then hurrying away into the dim interior of the restaurant. I peered after him but it was too shadowy to see clearly. He entered a room but closed the door immediately, and all I could tell was there were men in there, for I could hear the murmur of voices.

I sat on the veranda. A waiter brought my drink and I tried to relax. Somewhere a bell clanged twice, probably within the church opposite. There was nobody about in the square. This was a very peaceful setting, a quiet arbour where time itself was at rest, summer sunshine warming the fragrant bougainvillaea perfume and chaffinches pecking at grain in the dust. And the bière was well chilled. But I couldn't quite understand what was going on in the restaurant and my curiosity was aroused even more when the waiter returned to prop up a sandwich board at the entrance. Entrée interdit, it read, séance l'Apicius Club. I was still trying to understand this notice when the waiter, hovering by my side, quickly removed my empty glass and vanished into the restaurant. Clearly it was time to move on, service was suspended for the afternoon. I stared at the sandwich board, fascinated by that one word – séance. What was going on? Were all those men holding hands at a table? Could I hear a faint knocking from the room? Maybe my benefactor was a medium! And who or what was Apicius?

I don't know whether I dozed off for a short time or simply grew drowsy in the warmth of the day. It was after all the siesta hour and nobody was about. I came to my senses and had to blink to clear my vision. There was a shadowy white figure moving in the gloom beyond the hallway, floating towards the room, carrying a domed offering in front of it. Was I hallucinating, or did it really have this long white head? Was this a ghost? Or, I conjectured, a fake ghost intent on deceiving the assembled guests? The door opened, and the apparition disappeared. The door closed, but there was a sudden outburst of excited laughter as if the ghost was welcome. Sitting on the veranda, peering into the murky interior, I tried to imagine the scene - and failed. Surely this was no spiritualists' gathering any more than a secret Mafia reunion with my driver the godfather!

I decided to explore. After all, I needed to pay a call and the toilet must be somewhere inside the restaurant. Side-stepping the sandwich board, I entered the hall. After the sunlight on the veranda it was suddenly dark in there but my eyes adjusted and I could see oil-paintings on the walls, panelled doors on either side and an ornate chandelier. It was more spacious than I had supposed. Heavily upholstered settees and chairs sat on the damask Turkish carpet. This was sumptuous, and rather recklessly my mind slipped to surmising this place could be a brothel. There was a door at the far end and I knew this was the room where all the action and the voices were concentrated. I edged my way towards it but dodged back into shadows when the door opened and the figure in white appeared, crossed the hallway and just as suddenly vanished through a swing door. He was hurrying and pushed the door so violently it swung back and forth three times before settling. I could see this was no ghost but a common or garden chef, wearing his tall hat and a long white apron tied at the waist. Above the swing-door was a notice: La Cuisine.

And then the door of the room opened and the man who had greeted my companion backed out, still talking to someone and rubbing his hands with satisfaction as he followed the chef through the swing-doors. The door was left open and I could see - what could I see? A table covered with a white cloth and places laid for a meal with wine glasses and glittering cutlery and men sitting round the table, eating from plates, except that they had no heads. Each of them wore a black hood which loosely fell to shoulder-length, but there were no eye-holes. At first I thought this must be some kind of Klu Klux Klan activity or possibly penitents punishing themselves as in Seville, but the hoods were black and the corners stood up like pricked ears. These black-hooded men could not see what they were eating. There was a weird chorus of voices sighing and droning, a susurration of ecstatic sounds, filling the air as forks, having speared some dark substance on their plates, were raised and placed under the hoods. I imagine they closed their eyes too as they munched the unappetizing lumps of foodstuff and perhaps they wore earplugs – for whatever it was they were sampling, they wanted to exclude any sense that might diminish concentration on their taste buds.

They could not see me, nor hear me for I made no sound but simply gazed in astonishment at the scene. The buzzing and purring undulated through the room, each person wrapped in his own rapture, transported to some other world. All this must have lasted less than five seconds for my paralysis ended with a heavy hand on my shoulder and a voice hissing in my ear. The door was closed, gently so as not to disturb the lotus-eaters, and I, with my arm twisted behind my back, meekly retreated to the veranda, apologizing all the way. The proprietor, for so he proved to be, was furious. I had committed a serious offence but he wanted to hush it up. Nobody must know – it was worse than catching grown men with their trousers down. I was dismissed with a contemptuous wave.

I shouldered my rucksack, still perplexed at the scene I had just witnessed. Strolling out of the village, standing at a vantage point to catch any lift, I brooded on the extraordinary lengths to which humankind will go to make their lives worth living! A beep of a horn brought me back to earth. A woman driver had stopped and was asking if I needed a lift. Once on board, I started to stammer in basic French how I had just experienced a phenomenon formidable in the village and when I mentioned the Restaurant and the forbidding sign at the front door she rocked in her driver's seat with laughter.

'Ah!' she cried derisively, 'L'Apicius Club!' And she began to speak better English than I spoke French; she was indeed the village doctor and from her I learned that the Club was an exclusive society for gourmets, that they must have been eating truffles, recently unearthed in local forests, and their behaviour was typical of men. 'Poo! Ces hommes!' she complained with a contemptuous wave of her hand. I asked about the word 'Apicius'. 'Ah, mon ami,' she said, 'Apicius was a Roman epicure in the time of Tiberius. He wrote a book on how to enjoy food and spent his fortune on rare delicacies for his table. Realising his wealth was rapidly going, he hanged himself, not thinking it possible to exist on such a wretched pittance.'

I have yet to taste a truffle. If I do, I have no doubt it will be caviare to the general.

Measure for Measure

As he left the classroom, she approached him with Bob Sparks grinning like an ape. What she saw in that oaf was beyond his comprehension. He expected finer discrimination from Jessica Long, one of the high fliers likely to make Oxbridge next year.

'The point about Bill Clinton is, sir,' she said, 'he had a willing partner in the White House. Not so with Isabella!'

'All power corrupts,' added Bob Sparks pompously. Ignoring the interruption, she waited for his response, gazing at him with those attractive hazel eyes. It was she who had made the link to modern politics, always welcome when he was studying a literary text.

'Willing or not, it was Clinton's responsibility,' he replied. 'Like Angelo. Don't you agree? '

The trio walked towards the Staff Common Room. The lesson had gone well. This Sixth Form class was reading Shakespeare's 'Measure for Measure' and discussion had centred on Angelo, appointed Governor and Moral Guardian of the City State. Nobody had a good word for him – he was a hypocrite, creep, rapist, cold fish, manipulator, seducer, lustful beast, a rather indiscriminating list but what most shocked the students was his ruthless proposition to the beautiful novice nun, Isabella, who was pleading for the life of her brother. 'Redeem thy brother by yielding up thy body to my will!' And then, they all chorused, he intended to renege on that promise. Angelo was undoubtedly Shakespeare's most detestable villain.

John Armitage, the young teacher at the centre of this story, could be well satisfied with his lesson with the Lower Sixth. Now in his second year at the school, straight out of university, he believed he had a vocation to teach. Never mind the glitches of middle school discipline, where he still had problem pupils, he knew he could enlighten and enthuse the students who were studying literature. As he thought over Jessica's remarks about Clinton, and the comparison with Angelo, he glowed with pleasure at the intelligent interest she was showing. Teaching was a great career when you taught students like her; there was something very satisfying about helping a bright young person to enjoy her studies. Picking up a set of exercise books for the next class, he marched along the corridor but his mind still lingered on the image of Jessica's smiling face. What an interesting person, he thought, seventeen years old and really stunningly attractive. The way she had laughed and given him a sidelong glance as she casually hooked her slender arm round the shoulder of that useless oaf Bob Sparks, made him shiver down his spine.

He was actually fairly beguiled already. He had watched her moving away, with a lithe catlike grace that made her buttocks slightly shift from side to side with each stride, and set her golden hair swaying, but what really captivated him was the frontal image. He had wanted her to turn and wave goodbye with a smile, showing again the undulating breasts under her jumper, and he recalled the way the peachlike skin merged into two rounded shapes that disappeared coyly. When she moved, they rippled and settled, the curve of each breast outlined, and her nipples tantalisingly evident through the cotton.

Something struck him on the cheek and fell on his desk. Stifled laughter came from one quarter of the room, where boys had been playing about. It was a paper pellet and he knew at once where it came from. He must have been daydreaming, in the middle of handing out the exercise books. How long had he stood there, thinking about Jessica? 'Hands up the boy who flicked this?' he shouted. There was silence but no one responded. 'Right!' he said, 'That's enough. One hundred lines each unless someone owns up!' Groans from the class; he knew it was his fault but he had to enforce discipline.

'Quiet!' he yelled angrily, and continued giving out the books. By the end of the lesson he had forgotten the punishment but he could not stop thinking of her.

The fact was that his infatuation was beginning to affect his teaching. The only lessons he really enjoyed were with the English set where Jessica sat near the front and was always eager and ready to start her work. He talked convincingly to the class, but his attention was often directed at her. The study of 'Measure for Measure' continued, and now he wanted the class to act out the crucial scenes where Angelo confronts Isabella before making a close analysis of the text. He gave out the parts.

'Jessica, will you play Isabella, please?' and she smiled, pleased to have been chosen. He looked round the class. 'Now who wants to take the part of Angelo?' Several hands were raised but he ignored them, aware of some deep-laid plot trying to surface in his mind. As casually as possible he announced his choice. 'Bob Sparks, I want you to be Angelo.'

There were amused murmurs round the room, and Bob Sparks sat up sharply for he was rarely chosen to play lead roles. Sitting in a circle the play reading began. Jessica was indeed a perfect Isabella, innocent, virginal, passionate, speaking her lines with a real understanding of the dramatic situation. John Armitage could close his eyes and imagine her dressed as a nun kneeling before the severe, superior figure of Angelo. He could listen to her all day. But Bob Sparks was awful, uncouth and stumbling with a monotonous voice that made Angelo stupid. John Armitage silently raged: the boy was ruining the scene. Why had he chosen Bob Sparks? He could bear it no longer.

'Stop!' he cried. 'Angelo is a cultured man, sensitive and high-minded. Excuse me, Bob, I am taking you off the part.' He was becoming aware of concealed motivation as he looked round the room, and then, suddenly averting his eyes, he announced, 'I shall play Angelo myself and we'll act the scene properly!' Firmly he placed the teacher's chair on a dais and sat down. Then, facing Jessica he said, 'You must enter the room as Isabella, and kneel before me.'

It was quite effective as an improvised performance. They acted the two characters with inspired conviction, student and teacher reacting dramatically to the situation, talented enough to express some of the complex responses in the dialogue. At the end of the lesson, the class applauded loudly, even Bob Sparks coming forward to congratulate the two of them. For John Armitage this was a new experience. Playing Angelo to Jessica's Isabella had made him feel immensely powerful and at the same time vulnerable to the attractions of this young girl. He found himself muttering lines when he was on his own:

'What's this? What's this? Is this her fault or mine?

The tempter or the tempted: who sins most?

Ha, not she. Nor doth she tempt; but it is I

That, lying by the violet in the sun,

Do as the carrion does, not as the flower,

Corrupt with virtuous season.'

As the plot developed, he identified with Angelo's secret lusts and his tormented guilt, the acceptance of hypocrisy and his cynicism. As he confronted Isabella he felt he had never been so intimate with a female in all his life. His had been a lonely adolescence and during his years at university he had retained an old-fashioned romantic patronage of the opposite sex which was based partly on an assumption of masculine superiority. He loved sport and although his physique was slight, he had prospered in both rugby and cricket teams and had not bothered much about women. Mainly, though, it was his lack of sexual experience that contributed to this intense identification, which sometimes left him fantasising about his relationship to Isabella and Jessica. He was careful to draw back from too much drama in the classroom, at least as far as 'Measure for Measure' was concerned. He allowed Bob Sparks to take over the role again. Jessica dug deeply into Isabella's character but understandably she was not drawn closer to John Armitage through Angelo. In fact, as she continued to play Isabella during later classroom scenes, she was tempted to wonder if perhaps she should be applying for RADA, not university entrance.

Essays of course had to be written by the students and John Armitage kept a firm check on the workload. Students had to choose from a list of titles on 'Measure for Measure' and hand in their essays on time. Even Bob Sparks managed to keep to the schedule but for some reason Jessica had not completed her last assignment, an essay on the title 'Equity and Justice in Measure for Measure'. One afternoon, just as school lessons were ending, she stopped him in the corridor and asked if she could now hand in her essay. He told her to bring it to the English office and he sat there marking papers, waiting for her arrival.

There was no plan, it was simply that he was alone and he wanted to talk to her. She knocked at the door, and entered, full of apologies for delaying the delivery of her essay. He suggested that she should read her essay to him, there and then, and though a little surprised, she was pleased to do this, confident that her work was worth hearing. Sitting in a chair by his desk, her brief case beside her, she bent forward to take out the essay. She was wearing a simple white blouse with a curving neckline that exposed the summer tan of her skin and covered the breasts quite loosely. He could see them rise and fall lightly and rhythmically as she moistened her lips with the tip of her tongue. When she began speaking, her voice was gentle, nervous and melodic. He was aware of her breasts being cunningly lifted by some supportive bra which made her flesh rise like twin symmetrical orbs. He felt an alarming urge to lean forward and rip the bodice away, to expose the superb rounded form of her breasts, to feast on the delicate nipples at their centre.

Did she realize what he was thinking? That the play he was interested in was the play of two firm breasts under her simple white blouse? Was that a sidelong glance as she started to read? Was she blushing under his fixed gaze? He stood up and walked away from the desk. She stopped but he told her to read on, as he moved silently behind her and studied her golden hair casually combed over the nape of her neck. Gently he touched a lock of the hair and she seemed not to notice. He could peer over and see the compact breasts nestling in the bra cups.

Suddenly he found his hands resting on her shoulders, slowly stroking the bone structure under her skin. Her warm flesh rose and fell more abruptly. He closed his eyes and gave himself up to physical sensations, unable to stop his fingers from reaching the swelling breasts and cradling them as he gently plunged lower. Some kind of energy seemed to pass between his palms and the soft texture of her breasts, a tingling that suffused his whole body. She stiffened and then relaxed her body, as if submitting to his touch. His fingertips found the nipples, small and taut, and he began to caress them. He circled gently and delicately over the silky flesh that pulsed softly as he explored.

He was conscious of powerful stirrings in his crotch as his member tried to rise and he had to shift position to allow a comfortable tumescence. He leaned over her, arms extended, and she seemed to incline her head so he could inhale the honey fragrance of freshly shampooed hair. She was sighing, no longer reading, the essay falling to the floor. He gradually became aware that something was crawling across his right thigh, moving towards his crotch. She had bent her elbow behind her back and now her hand was stealthily creeping towards the rigid mound of his erection, fingers seeking an entrance via the slick downward pull of the zip fastener. He came to with a jolt.

She was no Isabella, no innocent virgin! She must know what she was doing. She was way ahead of him. He felt as if a rug was being pulled from under him. Confidence tottered and he drew back. She sat motionless, clasping her hands, bowing her head so that the golden shower of hair obscured her face.

'I am sorry,' he heard himself say, 'Terribly sorry. What came over me?'

She bent to pick up the essay, her face still concealed. What was she thinking? How would she react? Suddenly the enormity of what had happened overwhelmed him. He sat down at his desk, shaking. He had betrayed the trust between teacher and pupil, taken advantage of a girl in his charge, given way to vile lust and intimacy. He would lose his job, his reputation destroyed, he would be imprisoned for assault, abuse …

'Shall I leave the essay, sir?' Jessica asked. She was standing, facing him, tidying the neckline of her blouse, looking at him with bright hazel eyes, a halo of golden curls, and totally enigmatic in expression.

'Yes, thank you, Jessica,' he muttered feebly. He couldn't look at her, he took the essay with shaking hands. What was she going to do? Would she go straight to the Head's study? The police? Her parents? Or would she denounce him to fellow students, ridicule his pathetic attempt to seduce her? She was at the door.

'Thank you, sir,' and she left.

He stood motionless, trying to understand. She thanked him! What can you make of that? Did she mean it? Remain silent? Bear no grudge? More likely, seek revenge or some kind of compensation. However justice was to be measured, he was guilty. Perhaps he should tender his resignation before he was sacked.

He staggered to the door. He could see her at the end of the corridor, talking to someone. It was Bob Sparks, gesticulating, arguing with her as they turned the bend. Surely she was telling him what had happened.

He was still holding her essay. He read a few sentences, as if there might be some clue there. He found a quotation, referring to Angelo's lust:

'Sure it is no sin,

Or of the deadly seven it is the least …'

Was there comfort in that? He couldn't bear to read on.

The Birds

He stopped the car and looked down the narrow road snaking towards a bend that obscured the village below. A man was plodding up the slope, a back-pack bowing him forward, eyes fixed on the tarmac, grimly determined to force his way up the sharp gradient. He watched the man pass by without so much as a glance.

"Rather you than me," he muttered, and eased the car down the lane in second gear. It was even steeper than he remembered as he edged past dry-stone walls and stunted greenery until the car reached the bottom of the hill, encountered cobblestones and started to rumble. There was an uninteresting inn where the road levelled off and turned a corner, and a few cottages and houses marked the entrance to Staithes village but now he was meandering his way along the only high street with uneven shoulder-to-shoulder buildings. Most were Victorian domestic dwellings, but Georgian windows featured unexpectedly in a few old-fashioned shop fronts with signs hung in their windows indicating "Rooms to Let". Glancing to his right, he could see alleys and passageways with steps leading upwards to sets of what could be fishermen's dwellings, but he was looking for "The Lobster and Cod" where he had booked his room. It was on the sea front but he probably couldn't park next to it.

The narrow thoroughfare suddenly opened up, like a screen pulled back, and he could see the open spaces of the walkway fronting the tiny bay. The tide was up and, as if in response, with the sun brightening the white-washed walls and coloured boards, the old sea houses along the front seemed to sparkle with the visit of an old friend. There was parking space for him, at least temporarily, by the lane. He noticed a blue plaque on a weathered old stone property with two bay windows, commemorating young James Cook, who ran off to sea from the grocer's shop nearby. "The Lobster and Cod" was just over the way, facing out to sea and looking like an obstinate limpet clinging to the rock at the edge of the North Sea. Even the battered door into the bar implied thousands of high tides crashing over the barriers and hammering to be let in.

He checked his booking with a plump, robust lady who ushered him up creaking stairs to a small low-ceilinged bedroom. She left him to attend to the customers below. Framed sepia photographs hung darkly on the flowered wallpaper, mainly scenes of maritime violence with huge explosions of spume and spray deluging the seafront. Through the casement window, he could see the two concrete quays pincering the entrance to the natural inlet where waves rippled over a strip of sand below the inn's ramparts. And then, like huge clenched fists from which these pigmy fingers protruded, the massive bulk of rockface cliffs rose up on each side. Years ago, when he was a boy, the family had holidayed in Staithes and he recognised at once that enormous slab of a sawn-off cliff dominating the little fishing settlement. They gave it an odd name but he couldn't remember what.

Memories flooded back but he was not able to enjoy them. There was too much on his mind. No longer a child, he thought, and he couldn't escape from the present but this place was secluded, a kind of retreat where he could relax and brood, taking time-out to think about his future and apportion blame for the past. Yet, as he left the pub to take a stroll along the little promenade bordering the bay, it really was like stepping back into a former age. The few cars parked casually looked out of place and visitors hung about with nothing to do but wait for the tide to turn. He filled his lungs with the fresh, clean sea breeze, remembering how his father had always encouraged them to take deep breaths on the sea front: "Now, boys, smell the ozone!", totally ignorant of the fact that ozone was a poisonous form of oxygen in the atmosphere.

Poor old Dad! He suddenly stopped smiling and looked up at the sky. There was a rather alarming outbreak of shrieking that previously his hearing had hardly registered. The volume rapidly increased until it was deafening. It was a complicated concatenation of cries, screams, wails, sighs and lamentations darting about the sky. Squinting in the sunlight, he watched hundreds of gulls weaving and winding their passage over the waves, wings outstretched as they glided, then beating continuously as they changed height and circled without touching. They seemed to invade every corner of the enclosed bay, shouting strange messages at him, their wings criss-crossing overhead like flashing white blades. The sounds, that had at first thrilled him, now seemed menacing and mocking.

Then, as if a decision had been reached, the birds closed rank and flew towards the rocks, landing en masse on the cliff-face. He realised the smudged and whitened surface of the cliff-top was actually made up of hundreds of gulls, all screaming like demented children as they settled on or near nests. It seemed like a seabird sanctuary on that huge promontory, and a colony of gulls was celebrating its successful take-over with massed choirs. There was something sinister in the cries that never ceased, the way they assumed control of the environment, totally ignoring human life below them. He felt the birds were snubbing him personally.

Fed up of the racket, he walked along the main street, glad to be out of sight of these disturbing presences, though he felt the piercing criticism of mocking calls still pursuing him as he explored one of the ascending lanes. Two workmen gave him cautious nods but there were few signs of life or for that matter fish, which after all was the traditional occupation. He read faded names on doorways, "Rose of England", "Star of Hope", "Blue Jacket" – once names affectionately given to boats owned by fishermen. Standing beside the old cottages, alone and quietly watching a trail of smoke rising slowly from a chimney, he began to relax. Until two black-backed gulls brazenly descended with a flurry of wings and started to stab a plastic bag left lying in the lane. Refuse littered the cobbles but they took no notice when he clapped his hands to chase them away. They fixed beady eyes on him and broke into a duet of keening, wailing and yelping that effectively asserted their right to plunder and scavenge. He retreated, as they knew he would. Yellow beaks proclaimed another victory raucously.

He entered the village-shop cum post-office, appreciating its old-fashioned medley of goods. There was a Staithes bonnet on display, prettily frilled with a stuffed crown for carrying loads on top. And little models of former fishing boats in Staithes, the cobles and five-man boats, the yawls and sploshers. And antique postcard photographs of Staithes Beck where the fishermen kept their boats and landed their fish. Almost by chance he wandered down a narrow path between houses and crossed the little bridge over this Beck. In the old days, boats were hidden up this concealed inlet, maybe by Vikings, smugglers, or fugitives. At the end of the pathway, he came to the towering rock-face and looked up at the massive buff on this side of the inlet. It annoyed him that he could not remember its name, and as if in response there was a sudden outcry of screams and jeering from a crowd of grey birds that rose in a cloud over his head. They started circling, as if mocking and inviting him to share their triumphism. Suddenly he was struck on the head, a glancing blow but the shock made him touch his brow as if warding off further attacks. No blood on his fingers but still a sore spot and he looked up warily, wondering if a bird was dive-bombing. He knew terns were capable of it but these were gulls, probably herring gulls, hovering over him and why should they attack? Then he saw one dropping to the ground to inspect a stone or rather some kind of whelk or winkle, pecking angrily at it. He had heard of gulls cracking open shellfish by dropping them from the air. Had one hit him? This bird eyed him coldly, as if blaming him for getting in the way, confronting him blatantly, beak wide open as it yelped and wailed. It seemed like a personal accusation. For a moment he returned the venomous look and then, realising the futility of trying to communicate, returned to the protection of the main street. It was time for a quiet pint in one of the pubs, away from this unsettling criticism.

On his way back to "The Lobster and Cod" he passed his car safely parked up the side road. There were unsightly blotches and splashes all over the roof and windscreen, some luminously white and others disgustingly coloured, like contemptuous graffiti. The final insult, which he would have to wash off in the morning. He was glad that sundown was bringing a temporary reprieve as the stars spread a dark velvet blanket over the sea. His sleep was troubled by the solitary cries of gulls, which, like guardians, still glided over the slumbering village.

The sun shone directly into his room next morning, waking him from dreams that seemed no more than confused and disturbing reminders of the past. Outside, gulls called to each other like lost souls wandering through his sleep. He looked out of the window and watched them wheeling over the bay, yellow beaks cruelly open as harsh prolonged cries floated over a muddy depressing beach, for now the tide was out. It was another fine day but he knew he would be moving on, leaving Staithes to its own devices. He couldn't stand the gulls' cries, the constant criticism of voices that mocked him, telling him what he feared was the truth, that he had to take the blame for everything.

Driving up the narrow lane that led out of the village, he wondered why he had ever bothered to come back here. Had he been trying to run away? What had he gained from his brief visit? Well, one thing was sure, he would accept the truth, admit his responsibility, try to make amends for the past, rather than endure the mocking gulls of Staithes. And suddenly, as if a blockage had cleared, he remembered the name. Nab! Cowbar Nab! That was it. The gulls would continue sailing with outstretched wings over their coastal domain but now his ears were closed to their taunts. He reached the top of the hill and drove over the Yorkshire Moors, resolved to do better next time.

The Swimming Pool

If you asked me which was my masterpiece I'd have to say 'Eagles-Edge' even though it didn't get me far. In fact things started to go wrong after that. In those days I was dreaming up really smart houses, not just crap machines for living in but beautiful organic artefacts close to nature. 'Eagles-Edge' was definitely my finest architectural creation; the only trouble was the client. He ruined it; he'd made money and thought he could buy my talent.

Early on, I remember stepping across the threshold into the skeletal hall and noticing there were diagonal shadows creating geometry in space. That was the inspiration for the interior layout and I planned a stairway sloping and curving towards the first floor - a cool and elegant touch. This was after I'd been commissioned by the Burnstones who had no idea what they wanted till I gave them my drawings. He left me to it at first.

Years back we both attended the local school, I guess that's why he chose me - helping an old school mate. More like taking advantage. He was a nerd at school, he couldn't do half the things I could and then he goes off to boarding school miles from home and mixes with the upper classes and learns to use cut glass. So he makes his pile and comes down from the city and starts snooping around. He's bought the land, now he wants a classy home built on it. Someone told him about me and he remembered the name. I knew it was my chance. I needed the money but more than that, I could design a really beautiful place for his site and get photographs in the Architects Review, to show that I mattered and I was good at my job. I fixed up the builders and it wasn't long before the foundations were being laid. Burnstone didn't come near the site till the walls were going up and then one afternoon he arrived and walked round the place, eventually stopping in this airy living room to stare through a window space designed as a stucco cream curtain wall. I could tell he was looking for trouble. He pointed to the three pine trees near the gateway.

'Those trees. I want them down, Walter,' he said, out of a cloud of smoke. He was smoking a panatela as usual.

'Don't do that, Mr. Burnstone,' I protested. 'Those three pines have been there for years. They'll break the flat symmetry of the wall.'

He driveled on about security; someone could climb the trees and get in the garden, as if CCTV camera surveillance couldn't cope with all that. What had he to worry about?

'My comprehensive design,' I told him, 'is simple but finely tuned, don't spoil the harmony.'

'Okay but who's paying the piper, Walter?' he snapped back. 'I want them down.'

'If you say so, Mr. Burnstone.'

I had to give way and keep to formalities. Calling me Walter was his idea, sort of familiar patronage but keeping a lordly distance. He'd gone up in the world; I wasn't going to risk a cancellation, this was a prestige job. You don't come across David Burnstones very often.

He had become one of those business men who pretend they're artistic under the grey suit, like they'll wear a flashy tie to show they're bohemians at heart. Burnstone went in for long hair pulled back and tied with elastic, though he was balding at the temples. Burnstone the buccaneer! He was slumming around the back streets making plywood furniture while I was at college. It takes seven years to qualify as an architect. The next thing I know he's taken off, floating Burnstone Bedding on the Stock Exchange and raking it in. You'd see his logo 'Dream beds for lovers' on the side of articulated lorries with a sultry blonde pouting on a bed. Corny! That's how he met his wife; she was modelling in the big stores, and he saw her stretched out on one of his beds. She's Angie Burnstone now.

I've mixed feelings about her. She's got a surface allure and I could tell she was interested in me as well as the house. When I was describing the layout and interior design she got quite excited, kept touching me and leaning over the plan, nodding and smiling as if really taking it all in but her eyes kept sending those sidelong glances at me. I had to be careful how I responded because

110

Burnstone must have noticed and I didn't want him jealous. So I flirted a bit with her, made one or two sorties which never came to a head, and concentrated on overseeing the building of 'Eagles-Edge'. To be honest, I was more excited by the erection of my dream house than anything Angie Burnstone was interested in.

I got the inspiration for 'Eagles-Edge' from my favourite architect, Frank Lloyd Wright. It was a steel and concrete structure thrusting from a rocky promontory with a view of distant hills to the west. It was taking shape nicely and every time I drove up the approach to the forecourt I got a thrill out of the spectacle. I knew it was good, and it was all mine. Well, until the Burnstones started meddling. They couldn't stop interfering, demanding alterations, fussing about details sometimes to do with the exterior surrounds, more often trivial matters inside the house like built-in cupboards that ruined the proportions or changing materials, colours, textures or fittings on the walls.

And then Angie Burnstone came up with a new idea - she wanted her swimming pool underground instead of in the open-air. It so happened there was a natural declivity in the rocky promontory on which the house foundations were laid. I had intended this to function as a cellar and extended garage space but, without any understanding of the mechanics, the structural stresses on the piles, and the weight of concrete above, she says she needs to get out of bed every morning, swan down the main stairs and disappear into her private swimming pool. I got pretty heated making a stand against modifying the ground floor plan and ruining the spatial balance. Burnstone finally took the panatela from his lips and growled: 'Shut up, Walter, bugger the aesthetics, just do what she wants. I'm paying.' And he poured himself another scotch. I couldn't figure it out. I remember her smiling at me, her eyes mocking, challenging. I got on with the job.

Anyway, my basement swimming pool was superb. It fitted like a hand in a glove. I had panels of coloured glass on the south elevation gleaming through the filters and the sides of the pool undulated and danced with light from the ventilator shafts. When it was ready, with the glinting water waiting expectantly, we watched Angie strip off and descend the stairs into a mother-of-pearl shell bubbling with aromatic oils, and then enter the inner chamber of the pool through a liquid veil. Exquisite! Burnstone raised his glass and toasted her lecherously. Not a word of thanks to me. He didn't deserve this work of art, or her for that matter. And then he criticised the entrance to the pool. He wanted my glass swing doors taken away and a solid mahogany job fitted, so he could lock the pool securely. The man was a cretin, a philistine.

'Eagles-Edge' eventually got finished and the Burnstones took over residence. By that time I was tired of the whole contract and I could sense there was never going to be a grand opening. They seemed to want a quiet life, with a dreary life-style and not even a house-warming party to show off the house. They didn't need architectural publicity and when I sent site photographs to the media, they weren't interested. Next thing I know the house is shut up for months on end, and they make only occasional visits. They never phoned me at the office. I heard about a few weekend parties from the woman who cleans for me. She'd been employed to serve drinks at some kind of orgy with my swimming pool used as a dumping ground for the stoned. I felt insulted. Talk about pearls before swine.

So I was surprised when Mrs. Burnstone phoned me. Would I help her put a statue of Aphrodite down in the swimming pool and would I choose the best position. I kept pretty cool but she sounded friendly enough and I didn't know if there was money in it so I drove out to the house. I hadn't seen it for months. It's a great sight, glinting on that ledge like some treasure chest with a dark mountain-side foil round it but I could see the place was neglected as soon as I drove up to the front door. My mosaic porch was chipped and the bell didn't ring. There were no servants; she let me in herself and once I was standing in the hall there was no charisma. Someone had painted the hall primrose yellow, and the mahogany door to the underground swimming pool stuck out like a sore thumb.

'Walter darling!' she gushed. 'Come and see my Aphrodite, I've brought it back from Cyprus!' She was looking as lush as ever, slim and perfumed, but I kept my distance. She'd been drinking, and wore some kind of flimsy outfit that billowed, making me wonder what was underneath. She seemed a bit strained, her face powdery

112

and haggard. Opening Burnstone's cheap mahogany door, she led the way down to the pool which still looked good, with reflected highlights dancing on the water. There was this statuette thing waiting to be installed, pretty tasteless, a kind of resin job sprayed in gold leaf but at least not a Botticelli look-alike. It wasn't difficult to find a neat niche for it. I started talking about backlighting but she was too sloshed to pay much attention. I realised there was more to this visit than fixing Aphrodite in situ.

We went up to the lounge and she poured drinks. It wasn't long before she started talking about her miserable life and how lonely she was, what with Burnstone and his infidelities. She was trying to sob on my shoulder but I can't say I cared. She had plenty of money; no doubt she could buy a toy-boy, but I held her hands sympathetically and murmured soothingly, all the time taking in the hideous cocktail cabinet next to my elegant mezzanine balustrade. I was happy to help drown her sorrows; I couldn't bear to look around. They didn't deserve a beautiful home, these bloody nouveau riche types.

I kept quite cool. It occurred to me that if I couldn't keep their dirty hands off my beautiful house at least I could have Burnstone's wife in exchange, there on the Persian carpet with a few silk cushions to ease the ride. She needed the emotional release; that was obvious from the agitated haste with which she threw off clothing. I quite enjoyed it, she was warm and responsive, sighing and moaning, embracing me with arms and legs very actively. My view of things was rather spoiled by smudged mascara and wet pancake on her face but that didn't matter - everyone closes his eyes when the climax comes. I was calm and calculating over each shuddering thrust, savouring the possession of this woman, enjoying my success over her contemptible husband. Each time I jerked forward I thought of an alteration, a mutilation, a corruption of my beautiful house and I avenged myself fiercely till I ran out of examples.

The next thing I remember is a sharp stabbing kick in my buttocks and Burnstone is standing astride me and shouting, while she screams and runs out of the room. And then I was struggling to my feet, trying to hide my nakedness while he roared his head off and grabbed a poker. He charged after her, and I could hear them running down into the swimming pool, shouting and screaming and splashing about. There was a kind of hollow acoustic resonance booming from below and then a sharp crashing sound and a scream.

Angie bounded up the stairs, her eyes blazing as she staggered through the door. 'The bastard's broken my Aphrodite!' she sobbed. 'He's trying to kill me!' And she collapsed on the floor, so I slammed the mahogany door shut and locked it. Burnstone was roaring and pummeling on the other side.

'He can't get out, let him drown his sorrows down there,' I said, leaning on the door. I felt pretty cool by this time. 'He's behaving like a big kid at school. You can keep him locked in till he calms down.'

Then, feeling pretty pleased, I headed for the front door. She'd be safe enough with the locked mahogany door. I stepped into the driveway where two cars were parked next to each other. Very comforting, I wasn't going to come between man and wife, let them sort it out themselves. As I drove away, I couldn't help thinking about the timing of events. If Burnstone had arrived a minute earlier I should not be feeling this exultant sense of triumph and power. I knew I had succeeded, well and truly laid his pathetic wife and felt really good about it. I'd scored; I'd shown I was better than them. Back in my office, I knocked back a few whiskies, raising my glass to the mirror each time.

Apparently Angie kept him locked in the pool all night; then there was a soppy reconciliation between them in the morning. Neither of them contacted me. They sold 'Eagles-Edge' for a residential Home, and I haven't seen them for ages and the last I heard he's into Supermarkets now. Pity about my architectural masterpiece, I've not had a chance to do anything like it since. I blame Burnstone. I'm sure he started a whispering campaign against me. He's been trying to get his own back on me ever since. That's why things have gone a bit downhill. Some people get all the luck.

The Art of Courtship

Trevor was making an effort this time. A tiny quark of energy had somehow flicked across his consciousness and stirred him to take action. He really did want to show Daisy he loved her but always at the last moment his nerve failed. Somehow he couldn't push himself when he got to the brink, something held him back. Of course Daisy was to blame too, she could at least show more encouragement while he struggled with the demons that held him down. Demons? He needed mental antibiotics, not exorcism, for his complaint. It was more like a viral infection that sapped his willpower and drained his self-confidence. It was no use expecting Daisy to boost his morale. She was hardly a psychotherapist, though reputedly quite adept on the couch.

Whereas Trevor knew at heart he was a couch potato, waiting to be boiled. In moments of self-analysis, watching the adverts, he admitted he was no salt-flavoured crisp, but that didn't mean he was a soggy chip. He had quite a reputation as a wit on the Internet. Usually he got through the day without being too self-critical but falling for Daisy had changed the situation. He knew a special effort was needed; he had to be more romantic, to woo her with tempting gifts, perhaps. But he wasn't keen on bouquets of red roses and boxes of Milk Tray or Black Magic, dinner at Spalding's, a visit to the theatre, a pop concert, perhaps an invitation to a weekend in Paris. He felt like some shady dealer offering bribes. And was there any guarantee of success? The more he thought about it, the more the spark in Trevor's eyes dimmed. The melancholy fit fell on him like a passing cloud and he knew there was no point, it was too elaborate, and he couldn't sustain the pose. He decided the only hope was to wait till he met Daisy unexpectedly and there and then declare his love for her spontaneously and passionately.

Quite by chance he bumped into her at the supermarket, their trolleys passing like ships in the night. She smiled at him briefly and continued shopping, leaving him to wonder if that little nod was intended to be encouraging. He ought to have called out 'Daisy, how nice to see you!' but the moment passed, she was disappearing round the corner. He followed cautiously and watched as she reached for a jar of horseradish sauce, her bosom brushing the shelves as she stretched on tiptoe, and his heart quivered as he missed the chance to stride forward to claim the jar for her. He realised this was the decisive moment, and he must respond to the challenge. He began to stalk her down the aisles, dodging the traffic but keeping his distance. Following her down a deserted aisle, he pinned her into a corner by the soups, using his trolley to good effect. There he poured out his confession: he loved her, it was fate that brought them together; they were meant for each other. He hardly expected her to ram her trolley directly at his shins and walk rapidly to the checkout. The pyramid of soups collapsed all round him and, picking his way through the tins, he limped back to his mother's house.

A wintry depression settled over him there and then, though whether the rejection of his love or the violent assault on his legs troubled him more was difficult to say. There was little change to his daily behaviour. A walk through the park was a daily routine, his one concession to exercise, only now he hobbled a little, every step reminding him how miserably he had failed. He took the path to the lake, pulling his scarf more tightly round his neck for the wind stabbed sharply as he shuffled along the trail to the Ring o' Bells on the other side of the park. He certainly looked a lonely figure but then he also looked not much fun to be with.

Trevor, recalling the dismal outcome of the supermarket declaration of love, closed his eyes and tried walking in a straight line, as if blinkering his outlook. Bumping against a park bench probably saved him from misjudging his steps and tumbling into the icy waters of the lake, which was the central feature of the park. Recovering his balance, he decided to sit down and think about the possibility of a kind of accidentally-on-purpose death. Not waving but drowning, he brooded, I was always too far out. But no one was there to mistake his gestures and Daisy would not have been impressed; in any case he didn't really fancy the shock of the cold.

He sat on the bench and identified with the emaciated reeds

piercing the cold patina of the water. Every now and again the north-eastern breeze stirred the surface to form rippling grey patches. Tree skeletons leaned over the broken banks of the lake, dark bushes huddled by inlets and a few ducks and coots drifted in cross currents, quacking inanely as if confirming the futility of it all. Daisy was beyond his reach, she was a modern Queen Boadicea who had charged at him in her chariot and all he could do was lie down and try to avoid being emasculated by her wheels. He sat on the bench brooding.

Everything seemed exhausted as he looked at the scene. It was as if nature had decided to sympathise with his depression. Nothing moved and then gradually he became aware of rasping croaks resonating over the water, as if some demented clarinettist was seeking new chords to start a wintry Rhapsody in Blue, only this was more grating, more desperate. Was there someone in the bushes? He looked around but saw nothing unusual except for a small dark duck with a thin neck and pointed bill paddling sedately towards him. The sound grew louder, more insistent, then there was a watery plop and silence. A cold gloom settled over him.

He was about to light a cigarette when no more than twenty yards from him something rose out of the shallow waters just beyond the small duck and in a shower of spray teetered on the surface like a fat trout dangling from an invisible fishing line, only this was no fish, but a white-breasted bird stretching upward with its webbed feet churning furiously to sustain the elevation. It quivered fantastically in a fight against gravity, sending spray in all directions - as if wanting Trevor to applaud, and then he realised the other duck was responding to this performance, fluttering its wings and squatting low in the water, its head pecking forward actively. What was all this about? They seemed to be identical birds with dark brown feathers and flashes of white.

Cigarette in mouth unlit, he watched. They were confronting each other, eyeball to eyeball, wings folded, necks held stiffly as the heads bent forward threateningly. He could see orange neck frills fanning out and black crests bristling like brushes that enlarged their heads. Were they having a row, challenging each other as they swung their bills backwards and forwards, emitting sharp clicking

117

noises? To Trevor, this looked like two males squaring up for a fight, straightening necks and threatening to head-butt each other. All puff and posture! For, as he watched, the birds twisted slender necks to peck at their own plumage, like two precious tango queans preening themselves.

And then, just as he sparked his lighter and lit up, one of the birds shot across the lake, leaving a ribbon of turbulence as it pitter-pattered away, while the other paddled on the spot like a marker buoy. Then it turned and came flapping back in a straight line, bouncing off the surface and racing away in the opposite direction, neck outstretched. Joy-riding or showing off, Trevor thought as he inhaled, and by the look of it, not worth the effort, for the other bird suddenly dived and up-ended itself, bottom waggling in the air. That made the show-off bird come to a standstill in a flurry of ripples, head ornaments and wings spread uselessly.

'So what?' thought Trevor, 'A ridiculous waste of time'. He blew smoke at the birds.

The up-ended bird bobbed back with a silver fish wriggling in its bill. Neck held high, paddling slowly towards the bristling adversary, it offered the fish and the other bird fastidiously swallowed it. It suddenly occurred to Trevor he wasn't watching some sort of martial arts confrontation but a weird kind of courtship.

The head shaking was starting again in a frenzy of staccato movements, the bills flicking from side to side and curious clicking noises echoing over the lake. Abruptly the birds turned and paddled away, then dived out of sight. All that elaborate movement and it was getting them nowhere. He took another drag on his cigarette. Time he was going, it was getting too cold. He flicked the cigarette stub into the water and watched it fizzle out. He felt thirsty, he needed a pint and he stirred to get up.

At that moment the surface of the lake broke with streaming ribbons and two heads rose mysteriously, facing each other and glistening with water, and two white-fronted breasts reared up, pushing together as if for mutual support as they ascended in magnificent symmetry, their webbed feet paddling like propellers and their necks stretched rigidly. From their bills hung weeds dredged from the lake bottom and they pressed their bills to each other as if wanting to exchange gifts.

He felt uneasy. Watching the birds tread water furiously like this, slowly revolving, breasts pressed together, two birds dancing on the surface of the lake in January, with a cold wind whipping up a flurry of spray and making his eyes water, he felt out of place. He couldn't make sense of it. It wasn't what he was expecting.

Eventually the birds calmed down, floating close to each other, heads waggling and ruffs opening as they slowly paddled behind a bend in the bank. And that was it, the show was over and there was nothing more for public display as they got lost in the reeds, with a rheumy mist settling over the lake.

He lit another cigarette and watched the smoke rise and vanish into thin air. Funny thing nature. Whatever had possessed those ducks to behave like that? As he walked away from the lake, he felt a twinge from his shins. He needed a drink.

No sign of the birds now. The water was calm as if frozen, reflecting tree branches like ghosts. He yawned. At the Ring o' Bells, would he sit at the bar and talk to Joe the barman or take a seat by the log fire? He needed warming up, maybe the fire was best today. He thought about the birds on the lake. Joe wouldn't believe him; he wouldn't be interested anyway. Funny kind of carry-on in the middle of winter, all that energy used up trying to get a mate - it didn't bear thinking about. He limped towards that comforting drink, shins still aching.

The Death Cap Toadstools

Wednesday 15 September

I am writing this in my journal because I am not going on with it, not in the way I started it three years ago, when I retired early from teaching thank god. I have decided to stop trying to be a latter-day Edwardian lady with ambitions to publish her record of local flora and fauna in words and water colours. I don't think I was ever equipped to maintain a serene outlook on the Sussex countryside anyway. Temperamentally I am subject to strong likes and dislikes which obstruct a loving observation of nature. I can't concentrate solely on nice natural phenomena in my journal. I've always been drawn to spiders more than butterflies, to snakes, not worms, to cuckoos not robins. That doesn't mean I shall stop putting down what happens day by day around my neck of the woods as they say, but in future I don't expect there will be much about the four seasons and all things bright and beautiful.

My friend Gwen says it's the menopause but that's long past. Actually I have felt like this for a month now - I know it's because I am depressed but it's not just finding everything goes grey that affects me. Sometimes I begin to get really hot all over and I feel this burning sensation like acid spilling over my skin. I try to scratch it but there's nothing there, just this growing conviction that I have to pay back Elsie Lanchester. I know when it all started but looking back, I don't think I ever made a vow, not really, it wasn't like a voice booming at me. I just said to myself: 'Bide your time, and stick your dagger into Elsie Lanchester when the time is ripe.' Not literally of course.

Another thing about going on writing is I can listen to myself. I've got to think what's what and if there really is something leading me on - I mean, concerning what I found growing in the wood this afternoon. It wasn't like me to go down that path. Usually I take Patch through the spinney and along the cart-track to the fields, he can chase rabbits that way, but for some reason I turned left and went down the path to the coppice and along the dry stream-bed into the thicket of young beeches. I don't need to write that down, I know exactly where to find them but I am thinking of the way I seemed to be led down that straggling track as if I was being taken to see them growing there, hidden behind the creeping blackberry bushes, sticking up between ferns and moss. I can't be sure they are what I think they are.

Tomorrow I'll go into the village to check them, the library opens at ten. (Idea!) Why not go round to Elsie Lanchester's and ask her to find Fungi on the Internet, clever-clogs would enjoy showing off her husband's skills. (Silly idea! That would give the game away.) What game? I can't think straight.

Planted new rows of marjoram and fennel today. Mustn't forget to water them first thing tomorrow.

Thursday 16 September

It rained last night so didn't bother.

I was right. The Latin name is <u>aminita phalloides</u> - sounds disgusting. There was a description of them in this book but they ought to see them growing where I saw them, with wild violets and anemones just round the corner and then this patch of shining knobs sticking up, some of them six inches high. The book said yellowish-green, but they looked white to me, deathly pale, about twenty of them looking like soft meringues full of E-coli germs.

Have spent most of day thinking about them. They look evil. How did they get there? Why me?

Saturday 18 September

Went down to where the you-know-what are. No different, except more of them, I think. Nobody to disturb them, funny how other things can live next to them.

Went to WI this afternoon. EL in the chair, getting laughs, if only they knew what she had done they'd laugh on the other side of their faces.

Apart from that, what's wrong with Elsie Lanchester?

She is a snob - she is a bully - she is a know-all - she is a hypocrite - she talks too loudly - she speaks like a female Colonel - she has no manners - she has no taste - she is stout and struts on fat legs - she is a cheat

Can't go on, won't get to sleep with all this thinking.

Monday 20 September

Took Patch rabbiting up by the fields, didn't want to go down that path today. Spent most of afternoon potting herbs to take to Garden-Centre in the morning - why the sudden demand for Basil? Has Delia Smith been at it again?

Need to change trade name, says Mr. Cartwright: 'Sussex Culinary Herbs' doesn't sell. He suggests 'Chanctonbury Magic'. I said, 'They'll think I am a witch, Mr. Cartwright!'

Have just read through my Hate-list. How petty-minded to object to Elsie Lanchester because she is tubby, sloppy, vulgar, common, sly and lying. No, I don't need a list to remind me why I hate her. She robbed me, that's enough.

Tuesday 21 September

Went to Garden Centre with 40 punnets. Got paid - good but saw that Lanchester woman buying herbs, nearly rushed over to reclaim mine. Typical condescension, 'How nice to see you!' then turning a cold shoulder on me. Guilty conscience.

Norma Gibbs says the Lanchesters are going to Tuscany for a month, and Mrs. Lanchester let her look round the new conservatory they've just put up - no expense spared, it seems, lots of garden furniture and exotic palms. Must have cost them a fortune. Well, we know where that came from, but I couldn't say anything to Mrs. Gibbs, she would only start gossiping and I can't prove anything because it's between Elsie Lanchester and me. Everyone would think I was just being envious, which I am not, I wouldn't want to be Elsie Lanchester in a month of Sundays, not with her conscience poisoning her, not that anyone would know. Impervious to guilt, she is.

I think I shall take a bag down the wood and pick those Death Cap toadstools tomorrow. I've got an idea.

Full moon through my bedroom window, the ivy on the cottage wall gleams silver. I can see the trees on Chanctonbury Ring silhouetted, like a long barrow on top of the downs. It's all very still, there's a fox screaming in the thicket. If you go into the woods tonight, you'd better go in disguise!

I'll go first thing, while nobody's about.

Wednesday 22 September

They've gone! Just a few rotting fibres on the moss, nothing to pick. I thought at first someone had taken them but no, there would be shoe-prints and broken stems. That's nature for you, just when you decide on action it snatches the means from you. Why tempt me and then thwart me?

I must write it down otherwise it's burning a hole in my head. She had no right to switch those tickets. She is a cheat, a hypocrite. I don't suppose she planned it for that Saturday, it was no different and she seemed the same as usual, we went in her Volvo to the Supermarket near the town, did our shopping and ended up buying our Lottery tickets. We were thick as thieves (that's a good one!) up till then, always sat next to each other on the coach outings, people used to call us Little and Large on account of our different physique. I've always been slim, being portly she envied me my sylphlike form. She lives in the big house and my little cottage is at the corner of their four acres, so we are neighbours and we both take an interest in the W.I. She used to respect me for being a teacher. I may not have much money but I had contentment and happiness at my green fingertips - so she said. And I felt sorry for her being stuck with that starchy, superior-sounding husband. 'Wish I had your independence,' she would say. Well, it isn't all fun and games on my pension, I could have done with a windfall.

We got a pound lottery ticket each every Saturday, we weren't expecting to win a million but it felt we were livening things up a bit for the weekend. Elsie used to stick a pin to choose her numbers, so often she didn't remember what they were but I know what my numbers are each time because I am into numerology and I follow a system, my birthday number being 6 so I tend to choose a sequence like 6 - 12 - 18 and so on, or 6 - 8- 48.

That Saturday I definitely was doing a division order and I marked 42 - 6 - 7 - 30 - 15 – 12.

13 - 7 - 47 - 41 - 23 - 19. There now, I've written them down, the numbers on the ticket she said was mine - they ought to burst into flames on the page. I would never choose all odd numbers for a start, and as for prime, it seems funny she chose them with a pin. She's that devious.

Got to stop writing like this, makes me moody and I won't sleep without dreaming of nasty things which wake me up.

Thursday 23 September

Rainy all day, went for walk with Patch. Still thinking what it means if you see four magpies. 'One is sorrow, two is mirth, three is a wedding, four is a birth' - but Gwen says it should be: 'four is a death, five is heaven, six is hell and seven the devil himself.' She makes a cross with her thumbs at all magpies. Definitely four of them in the fallow field, swooping and fluttering with lopsided tails, calling to me.

And then a raven glided overhead, croaking at me, a voice as black as its feathers.

Mist over the Ring and raindrops dripping from branches. Have a premonition I ought to go down the thicket tomorrow, though it'll be muddy after all the rain.

Friday 24 September

They are there again. Lots of them! Patch took one sniff and his tail went down, whimpering and backing off. More yellowy green this batch, with white gills halfway up the stems and a soft ring at the base. I went straight back to the cottage and got the big basket and a glove. They broke from the ground easily, I lay them flat as gentle as I could in the basket.

The book said less than a quarter of a specimen can lead to a slow painful death.

Decided to test potency. Mashed one Death Cap in salt water, added porridge and rice and bits of liver, and I have left it overnight by the fox-run. Point is, if an animal eats it and doesn't drop dead at once how will I know what happened? Some mammals have a special extra smell organ in their nose-tip and that warns them. We haven't got that, so probably nothing will happen.

Saturday 25 September

A terrible day. Patch is recovering, thank God. I blame myself, I forgot all about the potion when I let him out this morning. He made a beeline for it, so it seems. By the time I was out and about, all the potion had vanished and I was looking for dead foxes, though when Patch started whining and rolling over I realised he must have wolfed it. It wasn't till I smelled this awful smell in the kitchen I knew he couldn't control himself. He had the trots all day, as Gwen calls it. I had to wash him down and keep him outside after that and he howled miserably most of the time. He was ill until teatime.

I shall keep quiet about Patch and the potion. It won't do for people to know I am experimenting with Death Cap toadstools. At least I learned something - it causes diorr/ diarhoe... Can't spell it.

According to Mrs. Gibbs, the Lancasters are going to Tuscany on Tuesday, flying from Gatwick. Three days from now.

Mr. Cartwright says did I know there were genetically modified herbs, and oughtn't we to go in for them. Didn't like his idea of a joke about Greenpeace pulling up our plants. I've got enough experimenting to worry about.

Tomorrow I shall be the guinea pig, not Patch.

Sunday 26 September

The Vicar said something in his sermon this morning about forgiveness. No matter what trespasses people commit, we should forgive them because we should not harbour grudges or resentment as these will cause our souls to fester and deteriorate. We should not keep our grievances green; he actually spoke of picking at scabs. I

126

thought to myself, 'Ho ho, Vicar, you don't know half of what goes on in your parish. Easy to forgive when you are ignorant of human depravity.'

I don't think she did it deliberately. I mean, we filled in the tickets and got them registered. She paid with a five-pound note and got the change from the assistant. She put the tickets in her purse and I forgot to ask for mine when we got back home. Admittedly I also forgot to pay a pound to Elsie, but that didn't mean anything because we bought tickets every week and would always settle up. But not this time. I was so busy; I didn't get my ticket from her until after the draw. In fact, I thought it unusual but she was round at my door fifteen minutes after the numbers had been chosen, asking for the money and giving me the Lottery ticket with the numbers: 13-7-47-41-23-19.

She had gone by the time I was checking these numbers and thinking this wasn't my ticket. I had no idea which numbers had won but I am darned sure she knew. Sunday morning I read the paper. 6-7-12-15-30-42 was the winner, four sharing four million and Elsie Lanchester was phoning to claim her prize. Not that she told anyone, she didn't want publicity, naturally enough.

I told her that was my ticket but she acted like she was shocked at the suggestion. She distinctly remembered the numbers and she had written her name down on the ticket. What could I do? Her word against mine. The funny thing is, after she had got the money, she never told anyone about winning a million. And I said nothing, not even to Gwen.

I said nothing to the Vicar; I just smiled at him as we shook hands in the church porch.

I have eaten a quarter of a Death Cap toadstool, mashed with milk.

Monday 27 September

Two days to D-Day. Was sick in the night. Felt a bit fuzzy but no serious effects. I shall go ahead.

Mixed two specimens into a vegetarian quiche, using mushrooms and peppers and liberal herbs. Baked it in foil dish and gave it to Gwen with request that she calls at the Lanchesters with it. This is clever move, I think, because she likes Gwen and has had home-made food from her before.

I'm hoping for a little more than sickness. Ideally she won't be fit to go on holiday.

Tuesday 28 September

Excruciating pain in the abdomen, thought it was appendix but they took that away long ago. Sweated and soaked nightgown. Should I call the doctor? Have put rest of toadstools down toilet, they were going mouldy. I feel awful, could be in for slow lingering death. Dagger stabs in my guts. Phoned Gwen but no answer.

Am lying on couch trying to write this clearly, my eyes keep blurring and head aches. I am very sorry for what I have done. If the worst comes to the worst, please look after Patch. If I feel like this with a quarter of a Death Cap, what will two whole ones do to her? What have I done? I deserve to die. The Vicar was right. And now I am being punished for my sin.

Wednesday 29 September

A miracle, I am still here. Seem to have slept for ten hours and feel better for it. Cottage in a mess but don't expect visitors.

D-Day for the Lanchesters. Wonder if they got to Gatwick. I'm dying to know what has happened, no news is good news, about the effect of the toadstools I mean.

Must have a bath, I feel so grubby. There's the phone ringing.

I feel terrible. Norma Gibbs has just phoned, very excited. I can't believe it. I didn't intend to kill Mr. Lanchester. The holiday is off, Mr. Lanchester passed away early this morning very unexpectedly. He was rushed off to hospital and died on the way. Mrs. Lanchester is distraught.

Dr. Finmere is their doctor, like me. What will he find? There's bound to be a post-mortem with the Coroner. I wish I could run away.

Thursday 30 September

Have decided, after a sleepless night, to make full confession to the police. I shall let them read this journal, so they can see it was all a huge mistake. Poor Mr. Lanchester, I hope he didn't suffer too much; I wouldn't want him to have lingered in agony. Can't bring myself to phone Elsie to offer my condolences but I really do feel sorry for her. One question keeps nagging at me but I can't bring myself to ask: did Elsie Lanchester eat any of the quiche or was it just her husband? And was any left?

A bombshell. Elsie Lanchester has just been on the phone to me. Very tearful, I couldn't understand all she babbled but she wanted me to know her husband has just died - and she felt very sorry about our little quarrel (little!) and she hoped we could be friends because she needed support in her hour of need. And a lot more between the sobs and the nose blowing. She said nothing about sharing the lottery money of course but she may have meant well, she was very upset. Of course I told her how sorry I was that Mr. Lanchester had passed away and I couldn't resist asking if he had enjoyed the quiche. 'Quiche?' she says. 'What quiche?'

Apparently Gwen didn't deliver it. Mr. Lanchester died of a stroke, not a stomach upset, he had always been susceptible and the worry of arranging the holiday had brought it on.

Gwen let me down; my best friend let me down. I have been phoning her for the last two hours and she doesn't reply. I want to know why she didn't deliver the quiche as I asked and where is it now.

Getting worried. Gwen doesn't answer.

Oh my God …

Daedalus over Sussex

Visibility was excellent; even observed through goggles the clarity of outlines and colours was impressive. The underlying chalk of the downs made surface detail stand out more clearly. He watched the sea breaking lazily into a succession of milky waves that stroked the land. Time was slowing down as a Connex yellow train inched its way through patchwork fields towards Newhaven; needling irrigation waterways were like silks threaded to the river bends; that distant ferry cut a creamy wake through the cobalt crinkled Channel, heading for France but he didn't envy any travellers. He was where he wanted to be.

He looked at the height gauge - 300 feet, and shifted position to swing the delta wing in a dipping curve, aiming to catch the air current as it passed the harbour mouth. It would take him over the Seven Sisters, soaring above the undulations of the cliff-top and then inland towards Mount Caburn. He felt secure under the great wing, buoyant in the fresh steady breeze, and sang as the aileron wires hummed and whistled. He had shaken off the shackles of earthly cares and leapt into free flight, though uneasy reminders kept darkening his outlook like cloud-shadows drifting over the landscape.

'As usual, sneaking off to play at birds, when you should be opening up for the holiday.

When are you going to mend the fence?

What about the washing line?

You're selfish, Steve, all you ever think about is that flying thing!'

His mother, always complaining. He had said nothing, just fixed the baggage to the roof rack firmly, and as he drove off to the launching site her sour face watched him silently through the kitchen window. She didn't want him in her house, a twenty-nine year old son still at home. He never should have gone back to her.

131

He loved that moment when lift-off abruptly snatched him from the ground, his feet still pumping at the receding ground, as if he was making a getaway from the scene of a crime. He was swept into the void, dangling and settling in the harness, hands gripping the control bar, the vast bird above his head pulling at his arms, making him weightless, carrying him effortlessly on the journey to - to ... did it matter where? The great arrowhead pierced the sky, carrying the archer who had released it. Once aloft, he felt immune, secure in his bonding with the Ragallo, safe in this partnership. Then a gull glided by, wings rocking to finger the air currents. Beak opening wide, it screamed at him, reminding him of Rachel at breaking point.

'I've had just about enough, cooped up in this place. We can't go on like this, Steve.

You're getting on my nerves!

We never do anything.

You don't love me. What you ever done for me?

You care more for that blasted hang-glider than you do for me.

I've got Billy to look after and all you can do is lie there.'

He had been a sitting target for Rachel's nagging barbs while he was hobbling about with a fractured tibia, the result of trying to land with a following wind - the leading edge had stalled and he had crashed. That had set him back, he needed a new keel and sails; money was short - paying for a shop-minder while he couldn't work. And Rachel not speaking to him for days, and little Billy not knowing where to turn.

And then the ultimatum. It was five years ago, but still as clear as the view over the coastline. Rachel giving him the solicitor' s letter, hiding behind the legal terminology, scowling aggressively like a featherweight sizing him up, lips pressed tightly, eyes unblinking, ready to deliver the knockout blow.

'I told you, I want you out.

You've got to leave, Steve, go live on your own.

I'm his mother; I need the house to make a home for him.

Sod off!'

Six-year old Billy holding her hand, sucking his thumb, not sure what to make of it all. Nor him neither, he had gone meekly like a guilty mongrel, tail between his legs and barely time to explain to his son, to embrace him and to promise to be just round the corner. Trouble was, he had been more than half glad to be on his own - for a time. Then, after a few months in cheerless digs, he had gone back to where his mother lived, widowed and lonesome, back to his old room and a home for the Ragallo in the garage. Big mistake to go back, he should have pressed on into the unknown, not tried to live in the past.

Below, tracks scratched and scored the downlands, indeterminate communication lines, and one grey road led purposefully over the hillside. Slung comfortably in his harness, he watched a column of smoke wreathing from the black mouth of a brick chimney. Two rooks lazily circled and rose, offering themselves to the touch of a thermal. He dipped the keel and approached, feeling for the uplift that would take him to a higher altitude. He thought about teaching Billy how to manoeuvre the glider, so they could share the excitement and the thrills, knowing there was a bond between them, feeling the boy's admiration for his father. It hadn't worked out like that.

'When we going back, dad?

I don't like it out here, it 's cold.

Space film on television soon, I shall miss it.

It's boring, dad. Can't we go home now?'

Billy's sulky face glowering at him as they ate sandwiches and watched the hang-gliding. It was a Spot Landing competition on a hillside, a 'bulls-eye' in the field below them, and fliers had to land with feet on the centre-spot. Steve had been preparing to launch when Billy said he was bored and it put him right off his stroke. He had slipped as he landed on the spot and his glider's wing touched the ground - disqualified! And Billy had not even been looking. After that, Steve took his son out only on alternate Sundays, by mutual agreement. He was able to attend more club meetings and fly further afield. Billy preferred to stay at home making plastic models of Spitfires and Migs. A certain Mr. Bostock was helping him.

Boring! Steve rose effortlessly under the wing, soaring on an invisible elevator. The ailerons hummed, the back edge of the delta fluttered and chuckled as if commenting on Billy's lack of interest. Aerodynamics! Lift, weight and drag! The thrust towards new experiences! He scorned his family's disapproval. Why, he was getting more support from the great wing of his hang-glider than he had ever got from his mother's bony arms. This shining sailcloth, stitched in coloured stripes, orange, blue and mauve, was more beautiful than Rachel's powdered make-up. But he was sorry about Billy. Maybe they could get back together, when the attractions of that slimy Bostock bloke had eased off.

'Hello, Billy, it's Dad here.

I'm looking forward to seeing you.

Your birthday next Saturday, I've got tickets for the circus.

What d'you mean, you don't like circuses?

Well, what would you like?

Oh. You're going to the model aircraft exhibition with Mummy and Uncle Frank.

Who's Uncle Frank?'

Bloody Frank Bostock, Rachel's latest. He felt rejected and angry. He had turned down the chance to run a training day for glider beginners because of Billy's birthday. That was six weeks ago; he hadn't seen Billy since, he couldn't face the humiliation.

Concentrate. The nose must come down before the wind takes control. Settle now in quiet command, delicately adjust, and finely judge the angle that leads beyond the hill and over the ploughed field with its warm air currents. He soared and his spirits lifted. This was one of summer's glorious days, enjoy! Every weekend, as long as the weather was favourable, Steve drove to meetings at various launching sites. The hang-gliding club was his lifeline, his pathway to the stars, his drug addiction. In the company of gulls, kestrels, bluebottles, bumblebees, he became a free spirit, a space traveller, like Daedalus of old climbing a sightless staircase to the clouds. There was a future in hang-gliding.

'Mr Steven Byers? Good morning, a lovely day.

Well now, the Bank has received your request for a loan.

We regret that security falls short of our requirements

Bilateral surety is uncertain.

We would stress the risks of such an enterprise make an investment by the Bank somewhat unlikely'

Steve sailed on, never mind the risks; he was quite capable of handling his own affairs, thank you. He wasn't staying in his father's small electrician's shop forever. The sun was dipping behind rafts of shimmering clouds, spilling gold and carmine. He glided towards it, bound for Devil's Dyke and a landing on the hillside. He consulted his gauges for altitude, air pressure and wind direction; no problems and the weather seemed settled. The irritation of the Bank's rejection of his application was brushed aside as he began his descent towards the downland escarpment that bounded the Weald, with a long ridge like a backbone sprouting tufts of hair, untidy scrubland of bushes and grass. Beyond, the downs rolled gently towards the coastline. He leaned to the left and shifted weight so that the great wingspan of his captive bird tilted to the right. He was curving to encounter the wind and leveling to maintain an approaching steadiness.

There was a sudden whining noise that seemed to buzz in his ear under the helmet, as if an insect was trapped inside. A flash of a shape passed from left to right, with an angry scream like a small missile. A glimpse of a flying tiny engine, slim wings - he realised it was a remote-controlled model plane.

'Bloody hell!' exclaimed Steve, banking to swing round in a circle. Alarm gave place to annoyance and then to anger. There was a ban on model flying machines anywhere near hang-gliders. Some damn fool was too busy fiddling his switches to notice the hang-glider coming in to land. The model plane, a streak of red, was looping and arching to make another approach, this time head-on to Steve. It suddenly veered up in a steep climb, engine whining, and swung round for another attack. He could hardly believe what was happening. He was being dive-bombed by this remote-control machine! Some idiot was playing a game with him while he was engaged in one of the most difficult manoeuvres of hang-gliding.

'Bastard!' shouted Steve, 'Wait till I get you!' He felt like leaning out to grab the stupid little gnat as it passed but this would be futile and fatal. Balance was all in a hang-glider; one false shift of weight and the wing would tilt and falter into a dive or stall. He tried to locate the person operating the model plane that was still buzzing him. The shrub below was thick and uneven; he could see a few hikers and one or two stopping to peer up at him, watching the model-plane flicking round in tantalising circles. There were two women with rucksacks who stopped to point upward, and then he saw the slight figure isolated by a clump of gorse bushes, standing still, holding a box and gazing upward.

'Gotcha!' cried Steve. His intention was to land as quickly as possible, free himself from the harness, and race across to the stupid oaf, making a citizen's arrest or some such action. He ought to alert the other hang-glider members further along the ridge. Why hadn't they seen what was happening? He banked and made a low swoop over the owner of the model plane, which was still buzzing around, in great loops and turns. It was a young boy, unaware of the dangers he was creating, but that didn't excuse him. And then came the sickening awareness that he knew the boy - it was Billy. He recognised the green jacket, the baseball cap that covered his face. Billy! His own son was attacking him with the model plane! A fantastic concept flashed through his mind - father and son, flying together but now roles were reversed, the son getting his revenge, causing his father to fall out of the sky.

'Billy!' he cried into the wind, anguished. He felt paralysed, unable to adjust for the next move, a silent scream in his ears, a pain tearing his heart. His son attacking him, seeking vengeance! He couldn't bear it. Was the boy alone? Where was his mother, Rachel? Was she there, urging him on? Or was it that Uncle Frank Bostock giving his son evil ideas? He hovered like a hawk. There was a man lying as if asleep not far from Billy. Was that Bostock? The boy was looking up, waving now and ignoring his model plane that nose-dived into a bush. Steve realised his danger - the glider's leading edge was rising steeply, any moment the Ragallo would stall and begin to fall sideways without lift or thrust. Desperately he pushed down on the control bar, forcing the nose down, fighting to give the glider some stability, losing height rapidly and the wing flapping weakly. The ground was coming up to meet him, he saw the boy standing open-mouthed as the great bird descended.

He couldn't regain control. Something dragged him down. He crashed, the keel snapped and he was flung against the sail as the wing buckled, which probably saved him from death. He lay there, ribs cracked, trying to remove his goggles that were filling with blood, aware of pain but more conscious of his mind thumping with the thought of Billy's betrayal.

'Over here! Care here, he's hurt!

Someone send for an ambulance!

Are you all right, mister?

Hurt badly are you? What went wrong?

Want any help, mister?'

Steve wiped his eyes, trying to clear his head. Voices in the distance, a blurred figure of a boy, shouts and calls, another taller figure looking down at him, the boy coming closer, his frightened eyes, his red hair, the greeny-blue anorak, it wasn't Billy after all. Nothing like Billy. And the man, not like Bostock, fat not thin.

'Talk about a bolt from the blue. We couldn't do nothing,

'e fell just next to the kid, could've killed 'im.

Blimey, he's delirious.

Look at him, he's not crying.

What's he got to laugh about?

His hang-glider's a write-off.

Anyone would think he was 'appy.'

The Pensive Pensioner

I'm sitting in me garden shed having a quiet smoke. I do this every day, rain or shine, puffing away at me pipe, I'm not a fag man, never have been. I suppose you're presuming I'm doing this to get away from domestic chores, I'm lazing here in me old armchair in the garden shed while the wife slaves all day in the kitchen. Don't you believe it - she's off to the Community Centre every day with her friends. And I'm not skulking out here because she won't let me smoke in the house. She's ash-trays in every room. And I'm not bored stiff with retirement, far from it. I enjoy a game of bowls and a pint or two. But I do like sitting in the garden shed having a quiet smoke. And a bit of a think.

Every morning I open the back door and test the weather. Slippers and cardigan today. 'Course this is after breakfast and ablutions. I ablute regular as clockwork. Then pat me pocket for me pipe, baccy and matches, and off we go down the path to the shed, stepping over the cracks in the concrete, ignoring the weeds and the leaves, kicking snails and squashing slugs if I can. I like doing that but I has to be careful about the slime. Don't want it seeping through the hole in my slipper - there's a hole in the right sole of me slippers. A hole in me sole. Depends on the spelling. A sole with a hole can't be whole. Can my soul develop a hole? A black-hole in my immortal soul?

You see, that's what happens when I come down to the shed for a smoke. I start thinking about me and the universe and the meaning of it all. What's it all about? What's going on out there? Who am I? Or rather what am I? I haven't always been so philosophical. I've become a pensive pensioner since I retired.

Mind you, there's always just one thought in me head as I open the shed door. I don't keep it locked, I'd only lose the key, so you never know what might happen in the night. Will I find a body in the shed this morning? A dirty old tramp with his meths bottle huddled in the corner? A suicide hanging by me own garden twine? A

139

woman stabbed and lying in a pool of blood? A plastic bag with dismembered remains? That's what teevee does for you. And the papers. A lurid imagination, and a guilty feeling about me past maybe, leastways that's what the wife says.

I open the shed door and nothing's changed. A still life with pots and cans, spades and rakes, sieves and bulbs, a few geranium petals scattered like blood drops, some dried-up dahlias and a musty smell of nuts and oil, compost and apples. And me old armchair in the corner. There's only room for one body and that's mine. This is where I come every day for a smoke. And me own private think.

The doctor warns me. I tell him he's got the wrong end of the stick. It isn't smoking that'll do for me. It's the thinking. He don't listen, he bangs on about the national health and the cuts, never mind my private thoughts. It's not as if I'm asking for help, I'm not going mad or anything like that, but I do have trouble with me thinking. Depends which way I'm facing, out of the window looking at the sky or down at the garden pots at me feet. I get drawn into me past or me future, down there with the worms and the subsoil or up there in outer space. I prefer looking out the window.

It's that Hawking professor what's on me mind most - and on tv. He's got me thinking about quarks and big bangs, multiple universes and the laws of probability and dark matter. I've lost me appetite for the lottery, what with Time bending till the clock strikes twelve twice over at the same moment, or so it seems to me. Choosing six numbers for the jackpot seems a bit trivial when the universe is on your mind. And black holes and Singularity.

I think I can cope with all that. I can sit in me garden shed and puff away, looking out of the window, looking at the sky, thinking what's behind them clouds, all that open space, all that emptiness expanding outwards with bits of matter gravitating and stretching to infinity and eternity. And all those other galaxies and universes. And those other worlds and earths in other solar systems. And the possibility of forms of life somewhere else. I can just about cope with all that.

But then I start thinking about some other pensive pensioner out there in some other parallel world sitting in his garden shed looking through his window at distant skies and smoking his pipe, and

140

thinking about me.

That's what sets me thinking. Is he like me? Am I him? Does he think like me? Does he know about me? Am I wasting time? Why am I bothering? What's it all mean? Why am I alive? Who am I? What am I? And I can't help thinking, and thinking. And thinking.

Yes, I smokes me pipe in the garden shed every day.

Printed in the United Kingdom
by Lightning Source UK Ltd.
108685UKS00001B/340-405